DELIVER US FROM BEAUTY, AMEN

Dale M. Fiola

*This Book Is Dedicated to Certain Women Who Have Inspired
Me Throughout My Life:*

*Charlotte M. Fiola, Maureen M. Ciulla, Michelle
Farrell, Vicky Murillo, and Angelica Reyn*

CONTENTS

FOREWORD

Deliver Us From Beauty, Amen is author, playwright, song writer, and attorney Dale M. Fiola's latest work of fiction. I have had the opportunity to read, edit, review and comment on his previous works of fiction, prior to publication, and Deliver Us From Beauty, Amen is no exception.

Like Mr. Fiola's previous works of fiction, Deliver Us From Beauty, Amen is set in the near future, where a newly developed technology (in this case, in vitro genetic shaping determines traits and characteristics before becoming a human embryo) has gone awry creating disastrous unexpected consequences to the world and to "normal" human beings!

The premise of the work is well-thought out from a technical, legal, and sociological perspective and is carried out to its logical conclusion -- at a great cost to many people.

You will find yourself gripping the book while you read, in an effort, not to be sucked too deeply into the morass that the genetic experiment devolves into. It is a classic peek into the battle between good and evil, and you will be spellbound while watching it play out.

WARNING: Not for the faint of heart! But it may be exactly the type of warning that we need in order to prevent such a disaster from ever happening.

Grab a hold and be prepared for the ride of your life!

Roger McCaffrey
June 16, 2022

PREFACE

Science has made it possible to select the traits of our children. This is all possible through gene selection and gene shaping technology that order up beauty, brilliance, freedom from inherited pathology and immunity from certain afflictions. Aging can be slowed. In the 2050's, the gene shaping results in some biological changes in the brain's hardware causing unexpected consequences. Society's reaction to the violence occasioned from those changes creates an endemic paranoia.

CHAPTER ONE

Burnt Remains

The night brought calm to the unsettled day that preceded it, when windswept hills dusted the sky and everything that lay below it with dirt and ash. The Santa Ana winds as they are termed made their grand entrance again into the Los Angeles Basin; an entrance that arrives several times a year. Arising from a characteristic high-pressure system located inland that spars with a low pressure center off the coast, they can ravage the coastal region of Southern California with intense heat and high winds. They are the "devil's winds." For the mid-2050's, it was a hot time for this season and for every season.

But that calm did not stop the orange pigment from streaking across the sky mixed with white and black smoke traveling out to sea. The fires have become more of a regular visitor with global warming, carving up the terrain with reckless abandon.

Not far from the campus of UCLA, a stately home sits perched on a hill with a panoramic view of the fires gripping its tentacles around this large expanse of land. The home is located in a cul-de-sac. An impressive 3-story home with a flagstone entrance secured by large iron gates. A long stone driveway leads up to the mansion.

At a point before the sunlight would reveal the devastation of the prior day's calamity, a boy sits on a sidewalk near the entrance to the home. He is not more than 5 years of age and unsupervised. He is playing with matches, intrigued at the spectacle. No one is around or peering through a window to see what the boy is doing. The house and its occupants are unaware of the boy's escape from his room, lost in sleep. The boy is free to do whatever he likes and doesn't seem concerned about where he is, the darkness of the night, or the fires looming in the distance.

The darkness makes it difficult to ascertain the boy's facial features but, each time he strikes the match and gazes at it for a moment, his face comes into view. He is a very attractive boy with thick brown hair that flows down over his face. Each time he strikes the match, he smiles intently. The broad smile brings a dimple to the surface of his baby face. He wears pajamas that are purple with a crimson collar. When striking the wood stick match against the pavement, he says, "they love me." He throws the lit match over his shoulder into a wall of Leyland and Italian Cypress that have grown to the height of 5 to 6 feet near the entrance to the home. He strikes another match and says this time, "they love me not," sending the match into the bushes. He repeats the process again and again, striking a match and saying, "they love me," or "they love me not," then hurtling the lit match into the bushes. The boy empties the box of some 50 stick matches using the same phrases. The Cypress ignite in flames and the boy's face becomes quite expressive and he turns to face the fire with a big smile. When the fire engulfs the Cypress, he backs away from the fire because of the ensuing heat. Just as the flames begin to burn part of the house, he laughs, almost hysterically, at the sight. He jumps up and down with glee. The fire consumes the front portion of the house when smoke detectors activate and a built-in sprinkler systems respond. The fire spreads to the upper floors but the Cypress act like a Roman torch and the sprinklers are little match for the wall of flames. The upper bedrooms are engrossed in flames and smoke. The boy's mom never made it out of her bedroom. The smoke killed her before the flames ever reached her bedsheets. The boy's father was away on business and the live-in housekeeper was able to make it out the rear door, whose room is located on the first floor after the sprinklers were activated. The live-in housekeeper attempted to gain access to the double stairway to the second floor where the boy's mom slept and the boy's room was located, but the flames had devoured that entry point. She wept loudly as she exited the home but was completely surprised yet startled when she saw the jubilant boy jumping up and down smiling at the burning home from the front lawn. She went over to the boy and hugged him.

By the time a local fire crew could make it to the home, battling flames elsewhere, the third floor was burnt to a crisp and had collapsed on to a portion of the second floor. One-third of the first floor was a total loss and the other two-thirds would need major reconstruction.

The fire crew notices the empty box of matches on the front lawn. Battalion Chief Dan Springer approaches the housekeeper holding the boy and asks, "do you know whose box of matches this is?" holding the box up with a plastic glove on. The housekeeper answers for the two of them, "We do not." The boy interjects, "that is mine." The Battalion Chief then inquires, "how did it get out here?" The boy answers, "I took it." The Chief then asks, "were you playing with matches?" The boy with a definite innocence replies, "Yes. I love matches." The Chief stares at the housekeeper, "was he allowed to play with matches at night?" The housekeeper responds, "we didn't know he was outside and we certainly didn't know he was playing with matches."

Battalion Chief Springer shakes his head and says, "this fire could have been avoided. Why did the boy have access to matches?" Mad, Chief Springer walks off disgusted.

Chief Springer is a gruff man with a slight facial overgrowth of what appears to be the budding of a grayish beard. He has extinguished many a fire in his day and fears with each call he answers his life may too be extinguished. He is most appreciative for the career it has allowed him though he has some misgivings that his lungs have taken a beating with repeated exposure to toxic fumes. He has been diagnosed with early stage Chronic Obstructive Pulmonary Disease and has had to report that condition on his annual medical check-ups. Still, in his early 50's, he does not want to apply for early disability retirement because of the label that will be assigned to his health; he does not want to be fingered "disabled." Further, he has not socked away enough earnings for any form of comfortable retirement. Thus, he has no other outlook than the outlook to remain employed.

Walking away from the boy and the housekeeper, Springer meets up with the City's arson investigator, Tim Lairson, who gazes at the scene of smoldering burnt wood, ash and rubble. Springer says, "did you find the mother?' Tim answers, "yes. She was propped up against the headboard with one outstretched arm. She was attempting to reach for something." Springer incredulously asks, "No, how could that happen?" Throwing up his hands, Tim replies, "I really don't know but that arm was seriously charred and fully extended when we found the body." He hesitates to add but finally relents and spouts out to the Chief, "there was something mystical in that bedroom and I can't put my finger on it." The Chief looks Tim in the face and states, "you better not put your finger on it in your report or you may be outside of a job." Tim nods affirmatively and states, "not my intent." Chief concludes, "good. What is your assessment?"

Tim offers his summary of the facts. "The boy, Algar Puccini, is a 5-year old. His father is industrialist Theodore Puccini. The deceased is the wife whose name is Heiday. The nanny is Rebecca DeBlaine. The boy apparently found an old box of stick matches in the basement of the home and concealed it from his mother and the nanny. Early this morning, he wakes and goes to the front yard of the house and strikes them discarding them into the shrubbery, igniting the bushes and setting the house on fire. In my interview of the boy, he admits to striking the matches but, given his youth, seems blameless of any wrongdoing." The Chief interrupts and says, "your conclusion is it was an accident?" Tim chimes in, "what else could it possibly be? How can you prosecute a 5-year old for arson?" Chief answers, "I look forward to reading your report," as he walks away towards his truck.

Tim watches as the mother's body is taken to the coroner's van. At seeing the sight, Rebecca breaks down in tears, sobbing at the death of Heiday. She had such a close fond relationship with Heiday and, to find that this is the end of her life, in such a tragic way, is so overwhelming and difficult to comprehend. She holds Algar tightly in her arms. As the charred remains of Heiday are loaded onto the van, the face of Algar comes into focus as he spies his mother for the last time and, suddenly, something most unusual happens, he breaks into a broad smile.

CHAPTER TWO

Arc of Tranquility

It was just a simple thought, a moment of reflection, that led Seve Aguado to ponder the point. His job duties as Chief Engineer for the County of Miami-Dade may have included these moments of musing but it certainly was not on "County time." This thought sprung from a dire need to find a solution to a perplexing problem that has intensified over the years. And, here he was, lounged in a restaurant on Lincoln Road in the heart of Miami Beach, that the remedy to massive flooding bubbled to the surface like a gigantic orca fighting for air after 5 minutes underwater.

It wasn't divine revelation stoked by the hand of God or by the appearance of the Angel Gabriel that descended upon him like an oracle but something more plain and simple. While having a dinner of branzino, salted roasted potatoes, and buttered succotash, some debris from an overhanging Banyan tree drifted down upon his plate. His initial reaction was jovial – was he going to be charged for these additional condiments? He laughed out loud, causing a few adjacent patrons to glance over at the man laughing to himself. But, gazing up at this statuesque tree, with prop and aerial roots dropping downward and laterally to create a huge network of trunks, branches and roots, he reminisced about a recent trip to Maui, more pointedly, Lahaina. It was there that he saw the Banyan tree in full glory. From one 8-foot tree planted in 1873, it has grown to a height of 60 feet and has rooted into 16 major trunks with a unified canopy of 2 acres.

From that Banyan tree his mind floated like soft clouds over the Atlantic Ocean to the plight that has afflicted homeowners and resort establishments with rising tides and flooding. What could be done to stem that rise or cool that global warming to save Miami Beach, and its larger namesake, Miami, from this natural extinction?

Then, the kernel of an idea popped into his conscious mind. Connect a series of concrete wharfing several miles from the shore. He had some limited experience with laying concrete underwater in the Miami area but more akin to a bayfront construction and not a direct challenge to the ocean's currents. This would not be an uncomplicated task. It would require personal hours of work to lay the groundwork for its development. He had no choice. The escarpments placed between the shore and the hotels provided little protection when they had been worn away over the last 15 years. The revamping of those escarpments was now a lost cause. Resort owners were told that the first two floors had to be abandoned and retrofitted so that entrances would occur on the third floor and the elevator system rebuilt. The expense was astronomically off the charts. The owners rebelled in kind.

Seve was a visionary, first and foremost. His credentials proved that. He excelled in mathematics in high school and earned himself a "free ride" to Brown University, Rhode Island. He was considered for a Rhode scholarship and was a semi-finalist. He graduated with a specialty in Urban Engineering. He was sought after when he obtained his Master's and Ph.D degrees from Princeton. The County calls him "The Prodigy" at the youthful age of 25 years. He chose Miami inasmuch as he figured that he would be a perennial "snow-bird" if he lived in the northern half of this country, so why not live there year round. But, since arriving 2 years ago, he was cast into the turmoil of rising tides.

It was on this night that the solution surfaced. The project would be started at the Port of Miami stretching upward toward the county line at Golden Shores. A cofferdam would be the bathyscaphe of choice, where a dry environment can be created so that concrete can be given a fair chance to dry. Borings would occur deep into the sand loam until bedrock is reached. Steel girders would be driven into the bores and supported by quick concrete. The height of the wall would reach 20 feet above the ocean's surface. The one advantage is that the depth of the water is somewhere between 17 to 36 feet. The construction would take approximately 10 years to complete, he thought to himself. The 14-mile stretch had to be given a name. He thought and thought, realizing that a wall would create more of a bay influence rather than an active ocean, he tentatively termed it the "Arc of Tranquility."

Seve's ideas were easy sells. He had celebrity "good looks" and a tremendously agile mind. Together, it was a one-two punch that most could not refuse. The Ivy league education didn't hurt either. He determined to propose the idea to the Engineering Department and begin plans of construction that would ultimately be presented to the Board of Supervisors and State regulators for their approval. He was uncertain what the costs would be and definitely uncertain how the Board would review the project.

That was the good side of Seve. But there was another side that was hidden under layers of intellect and moral judgment.

He is a manipulator. He can get the most ardent fanatical person to surrender his beliefs in a matter of minutes. He uses any means at his disposal to manipulate the result he desires at the time and place he desires it. During the preparation of his dissertation, he wrote quite cogently about human nature and the compartmentalization of their thinking processes. He wove into the discussion that humans like to place everything into a compartment and choose ways to think in a robotic fashion. In this way, he wrote, "they don't have to expend the energy to create and think, but rather choose the simpler path of life's trudging along and following one another like a 'mule train.'" One of the outspoken professors on the dissertation committee remonstrated Seve for this misguided view of mankind. But, one week later, that professor's view changed to support the principles of Seve's dissertation 100%, with his hands shaking and one of his eyes blackened, which he identified as caused by falling in the bathtub.

CHAPTER THREE

Dia's Deadbeat Dog

It may have been the seeds of discontent sprinkled over her short lifetime or metabolic changes brought on by puberty, but there was no mistaking it – she had made a turn off the highway of life onto a deserted stretch of nothingness. She is brilliant. She captures ideas like a Chameleon's sticky tongue unfurling and lashing out faster than a jet plane to snare her next meal. In her education, nothing posed any challenges, whether it was science, technology, engineering, or math. It was simple. It was always simple. Those that taught her found her to be passably arrogant but nevertheless an enthusiastic learner. Early on in her development she would make up stories fabled about a place called "kinderot." Deep in the story lines and characters was piteous misfortune. Children who fall victim to sad and tragic ends. Her parents misinterpreted the stories as proof of the child's creative talents but did not see the dark lugubrious nature of her stories. Those stories carried on for several years and when the themes recurred story to story, the parents told her she will be a horror writer when she grows up.

Her name was Dia. She was beautiful. Her black hair swishing across her shoulders like a swinging pendulum with each step she took. Her greenish yellow eyes projected out of her face like flashes of neon lights. Her nose was squared in the center of the verdant display, innocent and unsuspecting. She had heard that, in the 20th Century, women preferred to have one black mole near their lips. She was not blessed with that natural marking so she limned one in with eyeliner. That marking against a pale face made her the object of so much attention. She was gifted with a very decent stature, over 5'10."

Her mother just adored her creation. She was exactly what she wanted: tall, smart, good-looking, and, of course, confident. This was to make up for her mother's own lack of esteem and shortcomings. Her mother always felt that she could have been a little smarter and better looking, which would have enabled her to be confident. She just beams whenever Dia manifests her intelligence unreservedly.

On Dia's 16th birthday, her mother gave her a cute Brussels Griffon dog. Dia loved the dog, named it "Miserable," after her favorite movie, Les Miserables. Her mother soon became quite attached to the dog. After taking a series of biology, chemistry, anatomy and physiology classes, Dia decided to experiment with the dog. She used a gas anesthetic isoflurane to see how she could change his behavior. In one of her experiments, she overdosed the dog and it died. In secret she went to a taxidermist to preserve his body and mounted it on her dresser. She assimilated the sounds of the dog barking and wired the animal to move from a sitting to a standing position. All of this mimicry was undertaken to conceal what she had done to the poor animal. She never let her mother in her room again.

On the eve of her graduation from high school, earlier than most students, she announced to her mom, Sierra, and her dad, Eadred: "I'm not going to college. It's such a waste of time and resources. I can learn from the internet." Visibly upset, Sierra retorts: "You are such a good student. Don't waste the assets you have been given." Eadred responds: "Look, we've put money away for your education. Use it." Dia adamantly replies: "I'm almost an adult and I get to choose what I do with the rest of my life. Thank you for your support but education at a scripted college of choice does not interest me at the moment."

Reacting emotionally, Sierra cajoles her daughter, "what are you going to do? Walk the streets?" Dia laughingly retorts, "no, Mom, I got greater aspirations than that." Eadred, rising from his chair, states: "Can you list them?" "Not right now, Dad. But it's like a medical import/export business," Dia responds. "You mean like a medical appliance importer/exporter," sums up Eadred. "Along those lines, but more involving tissue," she exclaims. "Tissue," says Eadred with an air of incredulity. "Tissue, you mean like skin?" Eadred questioningly. "Yes. Organ development and procurement," she reveals. Sierra chimes in, "doesn't that require a medical degree of sorts?" "No. I'm not the developer; just the procurer," Dia notes. "So, in other words, you would be a body parts procurer," he concludes. Curtly, she answers, "yes." Sierra worriedly asks, "what about your commitment letter to MIT?" "I'll rescind it," Dia answers. "You are making a big mistake, lady," says Eadred. Trying to use slow dissuasion, Sierra councils Dia, "take your time and think this through before you rescind." "I've made up my mine. I'm not going," finalizes Dia.

CHAPTER FOUR

Enbryo's Offerings

The couple is led to a conference room by a fashionable receptionist whose tailored dress suit radiates in colors of blue and yellow. She is very attractive and long legged from her topsy blonde to her bottomsy black heels. She is here to sell. Sell the product that her employer is pushing. "Have a seat and the video should begin momentarily," she states to the couple. "Can I serve you any beverages and treats before it begins?" she utters. The couple a little uncertain about the whole concept, simply nod in the receptionist's direction causing the receptionist to make a smothered chuckle. "Coffee, then?" she says. The couple in unison say, "yes." The receptionist leaves and shortly returns with the coffee. She replies, "enjoy your coffee" and then exits.

The video commences and it opens with an adorable baby smiling and crawling around. The announcer narrates:

"You may not know it but to look at this baby you would not believe that this baby underwent genetic shaping. The shaping occurred before the child was placed in utero and before the egg and sperm united to create a zygote. Here, at Enbyro Genetic Guidance (EGG), we can pre-set and pre-order the gene pool of your perfect child. If you want your child to have blue eyes, blonde hair, be tall, good-looking and, on top of it, brilliant, we can fuse those genes into the selected gene pool you desire. We can, through genetic redesigning, make your cute baby immune to most diseases, rendering obsolete many vaccinations and immunizations. We can turn on the genetic switch that plays a significant role in slowing the aging process and reducing fat accumulation. Frankly, we have stumbled upon a process in which the person will never go gray and wrinkling will be diminished to barely perceptible. EGG wants to make your baby perfect for you and your family. To make your perfect family, join our family of specialists and geneticists today."

After the video presentation, the Receptionist rejoins the couple. "How was it?" the Receptionist asks. The couple respond, "interesting." On cue, the Receptionist says, "I meant the coffee." The couple and the Receptionist laugh. The couple answer together, "good." Receptionist inquires, "do you have any questions?" The couple, Paula Cervantes and Naomi Tigras, are an Hispanic couple that have contemplated having children for some time but their financial position placed that out of reach. They determined that if implantation was going to occur, they might as well go all the way and genetically shape that first child. They have raised enough money to meet that investment.

Paula has a somewhat broken English accent sprinkled with some Spanish but she can get the message over. "We have questions about the shaping process and side effects," she states. "Those are typical questions that people ask about that our Geneticist, Dr. Marjorie Birmbaum, can answer. She can answer your questions now, if you would like," says the Receptionist. Paula and Naomi nod affirmatively.

Receptionist takes them down a corridor and they enter the lavish offices of Dr. Birmbaum. She sits at her desk and rises to greet Paula and Naomi. "Hi, I'm Dr. Birmbaum. Have a seat." Both ladies sit down. Dr. Birmbaum goes to the front of the desk and shakes both ladies' hands and says, "I understand you have some questions." She is middle-aged, small framed and of short stature. Her voice has a distinct songbird clarity as if she were belting out an opera at the Met. Naomi with a better command of English takes the lead.

Naomi asks, "do we go through genetic coding to make sure that our genetic characteristics will pass to the child?" "Yes," says Birmbaum, "we need to make sure the genetic pool comprises most of the genotype you desire. The one problem is that you both have different pools of genes. You can shape into child's pool those favorable traits of one parent and isolate out the negative ones. Then, when you reach a consensus on what traits you wish from each parent, we then, at Enbryo, will create the gene pool for your child.

Naomi then asks, "can Enbryo make the exact hair color and eye color that we want?" Birmbaum with a cautious look says, "we aim to get exact, but sometimes Mother Nature takes charge and we are surprised." Paula states inartfully, "blonde is brown, and tall is short." "Not really," says Birmbaum. "It just means that hues of colors are not exact at this moment in the state of the science. We are getting closer. What that means to you is that blonde may not be platinum but it will be dirty-water blonde. It may not mean 6'1" but it will mean 5'11." Both nod their heads as if they understand the Doctor.

Naomi asks, shifting her crossed legs a bit, "what are the side effects?" Birmbaum seeks clarification, "what do you mean, like birth defects?" Naomi says, "yes and down the road." "Our studies show that immunological results of genetic shaping reduce the likelihood of birth defects over an unshaped baby. But there is always that x-factor, that is an imponderable, that leaves us guessing as to what the ultimate result will be. That's why we call this genetic guidance. We increase the likelihood of the predicted outcome, but we cannot guarantee that outcome," concludes Birmbaum.

Birmbaum adds, "you are partners, so, I would assume that you are interested in implantation, right?" Paula says, "yes," looking at Naomi, who nods her head in approval. "Who is going to carry the baby full term?" asks Birmbaum. Naomi answers, "I am." "If you are going to implant, you might as well give that baby the best shot at being beautiful, smart and talented." Paula and Naomi laugh, both nodding their heads up and down in agreement. Birmbaum asks, "do you want to undergo Genetic Guidance then." Both Paula and Naomi say, "yes."

Birmbaum shakes their hands again and says, "we have some forms for you to fill out, consents to conduct genome studies on each of you and completion of your gene pool selection list." Both women exit the office.

CHAPTER FIVE

Business as Unusual

Sierra engages in some dusting around the house and tidying up as she goes. She goes to the upper floor and continues her way down the corridor. As she makes her way, the faint voice of Dia becomes more discernible. When she arrives at Dia's door, it is closed so she places her ear up to it to hear what, at times, is Dia's whisperings. She can't make out the whispers but the regular voice is clear. "I can't deal with sub-componentry. I purvey only the organs and what you are asking is not an organ. You want the cystic duct and the bile duct. Those aren't organs. They're ducts." Some silence continues and then Dia replies, "I understand that it is a life-death situation. You need the liver and hepatic and biliary ducts. I'll see what I can do." The call ends. Listening very attentively, Sierra almost puts her ear through the door just as Dia makes another call. This time Dia's voice has changed. The voice has taken on a whole different sound. It's quite a bit lower and calm – a calmness that eerily sounds like leaves dancing across a grave. Try as she can, Sierra cannot make out what Dia is saying. The only word was "deliver." She hears other mumblings and then Miserable let's out a bark. Sierra has not seen the dog for many months but she doesn't ask about it. Whether Dia is home or not that door remains locked to the rest of the world and Sierra is no exception. Attempting to listen closer, suddenly, the door opens and Dia exclaims, "Mom!" Sierra feints with the feather duster as if she is dusting off the walls adjacent to Dia's doors. "Just dusting, girl," replies Sierra. "Are you spying on me?" retorts Dia. "No, just doing some housework," responds Sierra.

As she begins to close the door, Sierra tries to glimpse into the innards of the room but can make out only little.

Speaking through the door, "how's Miserable? Haven't seen him in a long time." Dia answers, "He's fine. I've got to get back to work, Mom." "Okay," says Sierra.

Sierra goes downstairs and sees Eadred on the sofa watching 3d projections from worldwide news. Sierra sits next to Eadred. She places her hand on his thigh to get his attention. He looks at her and turns the sound to mute. "What's she doing up there? Everything is so secret," says Sierra. "She's paying rent so she is entitled to her privacy," quips Eadred. "If she's in the organ business, why is she so quiet on the phone at times?" poses Sierra. "It's her business, not yours," submits Eadred. With some hesitation, Eadred adds, "maybe it involves trade secrets and other private information." Sierra reasons, "come on its body parts; not the secret ingredients to a new beverage." "Have you forgotten, these are human body parts where people donate them in advance of their passing. There certainly is a "right of privacy, medical privacy, that attaches." Eadred counter-reasons. "I think it's wrong," Sierra concludes. "What is the real reason you brought this up?" asks Eadred looking eye-to-eye at Sierra. A couple moments of reflection pass and Sierra announces, "I don't think I know her anymore. My daughter has grown into someone else." "That's an oxymoron, Sierra, of course, she has grown into an adult," exclaims Eadred. "Do you want her to jump around like a toddler when she's 18 years old?" "No, but I miss that connection we had," Sierra sighs. In consolation, Eadred places his hand on Sierra's shoulders and states, "give it time. She's trying to find out who she is. When she does, she will reconnect."

Then, in a very quiet whisper, Sierra leans over to Eadred's ear and says, "should we have done it." He ruminates on the question and then says, "you ask me this all the time. Yes, we were right in doing this. She is attractive. Hell, she is beautiful! A perfect figure with an outstanding brain. She was top in her class and had to be advanced because she could grasp concepts with facility." He hesitates for a moment, "Are you having doubts again?" "Yes," Sierra replies, "should we have tampered with nature?" Eadred summarizes, "all we did is fine-tune the genetic process before fertilization. We put the sperm and the egg together and nature did the rest." Sierra listens for more empathy and it soon follows when Eadred adds, "look, you had a tipped uterus making natural insemination difficult. We determined to go with artificial insemination and do some genetic shaping. What's wrong with that. We had a normal baby with supernormal talents. That is what we ordered and that was delivered. Get over the guilt."

Eadred retreats from his last remark that caused Sierra to smirk. "Alright, that was a little harsh. What I meant to say is up to this time she has made us both happy, right?" Sierra thinks for a moment and then says, "yes," halfheartedly. "She was better than no child," Eadred postulates. And Sierra quickly answers, "yes." Eadred then proffers, "there is no telling if a child will remain close to her parents throughout her lifetime if everything was done according to the laws of nature. So, whether genetic shaping or not is involved provides no guarantees as to the child remaining close through her lifetime." Sierra nods her head that she understands.

CHAPTER SIX

Beat Up

At the 33rd Precinct in Manhattan, Sgt. Adam Peabody looks at a screen. He is a 54-year old man with graying temples and a general flop of hair that falls to just over his ears. A member of his staff comes in. "Daryl Craver is set up for report, Sarg." Sgt. Peabody replies, "let's shoot." The staff member jokes with the Sgt. Peabody and says, "You're unarmed," then laughs and exits. Peabody had little reaction to the comment because "let's shoot" is a regular staple of expressions he uses and he has heard that reply many times.

"Get a little closer to the screen, sir," says Peabody. "I need to perform some telemetrics before beginning the session. I will do a retinal scan and a DNA inquiry to ascertain you are who you say you are." "Okay," is the reply from the gentleman making the report. Looking at the results of the scan and inquiry, Peabody says, "you are Roscoe Mortimer, sir?" "Yes, Officer," is Mortimer's reply. "You live at "3278 Winglet Gate?" says Peabody. And Mortimer similarly replies, "yes." "Okay, then, tell me what happened?" Peabody asks.

Mortimer is a 73-year old male, Czech-Irish descent, with a full chested laugh and gray hair. He has been beat up pretty seriously with cuts on his face and neck. He is bent over as he sits in a hospital bed with a surgical gown on. He is a relatively short male, not more than 5'2." He has a penchant for tall women to make up that difference in stature.

"I understand you are at the hospital being treated from a

serious fall with cuts, abrasions and other injuries to your face, neck, arms, back and legs," sums up Peabody. He goes on to say, "please tell me what happened?"

Mortimer narrates: "I was seated in a restaurant called "Pouncing Tiger" having a beer when this extremely attractive woman came over to the table and sat down next to me. She just sat down. Didn't ask me or anything. She just sat down and looked me in the eyes and said, "you want me so bad." I didn't know what to make of it. I thought she worked at the restaurant and it was a practical joke, but it wasn't."

"I'm sorry to interrupt you but I need a description of the woman first," Peabody asks. "Well, she was tall, over 6 feet, had long platinum blonde hair that went down below her waist, and a very curvy figure but slender build. She was a white girl, not more than 22 years of age in my estimation." Peabody comments, "go ahead with your story."

"She says to me, 'do you wanna buy me a drink?' I was overcome by her that I stuttered at first and then said, 'I'll gladly dry you a brink.' We both laughed and she placed her left hand on my right hand and smiled. We had several drinks in about 1 ½ hours. I was beginning to feel quite comfortable with her. She had a certain sincerity that I relished. She was smart. She had a command over 4-5 languages and showed me she could speak Italian, English, German, French and Mandarin. She was the "full package" for me. At one point, she offered to massage the back of my neck. I'm not one to refuse a massage and I told her, 'go ahead.' It was that massage that changed everything. She told me she had a balm she would apply to the back of my neck for deeper penetration. She applied the balm to my neck which caused a chain reaction of hallucinogenic responses. I didn't know what was real from imagined. I heard her voice telling me to relax and enjoy the massage. I don't know if she hypnotized me or not but I felt under her control. Her attitude changed after the massage. She told me, 'get up and follow me.' I did as she directed. We went to a hotel room of her choosing and used a computer terminal to take a large sum of money from my account into her private account. Then, I followed her to the balcony where she lifted me up, kissed me and said: "Short people, you got to pick them up just to say 'Good-bye,'" and then she dropped me off the balcony, some 8 floors up. I guess she didn't know I had anti-gravitizer in my pocket that slowed my fall so I could survive it. I am happy to be alive."

"You should be," Peabody joins. He also adds, "did you get her name?" "There never was an opportunity to exchange names," says Mortimer. Peabody comments, "you had 1 ½ hours of drinking and you didn't get her name?" "No, we were lost in conversation about everything but our names," retorts Mortimer. "You have no pictures of her, do you?" Peabody inquires. "None. I know that's careless," Mortimer adds. "That's alright, just get real close to the screen and give us your best visual impression of her looks from memory so we can snapshot it." Moments pass, "got your best visual of her?" says Peabody. "Yes," says Mortimer. Then with a click, "we got the visual impression, thank you," says Peabody. "We'll run it through our system and see if she pops up. Thank you for the report and get well."

Peabody walks through the office and is met by another staff. Peabody says, "I want to show you something, follow me." The two go to Peabody's office and up on the screen is the last projection of the visual impression of the female assailant. "Look at this girl. She is a stunning 21-22 year old. What's she doing victimizing older men?" says Peabody. The staffer responds, "Isn't that par for the course. Attractive women prey on older wealthier men." Peabody quips, "but sex was not involved. They were just drinking and there was no overtures to have sex." The staffer replies, "that's what he says. He doesn't want to admit to solicitation." Peabody states, "run this through the system and see if there are any matches. She does not fall within the stereotypical predator profile." The staffer says, "I will."

CHAPTER SEVEN

Puccini's Algar

Theodore Puccini was grief-stricken with the involuntary cremation of his wife at the hand of son's own indulgences with matches. He spent some time institutionalized when his moral compass pointed downward to medicating his serious depression with illegal drugs. This resulted in his turning to women of the evening to fill the crater left by his wife's passing. Those pleasures were heightened by not only the freedom to explore them unabashedly but to reach new ecstasy points with a willing drug-induced participant. There were times he left for periods of weeks, passing off Algar to Rebecca DeBlaine to act as the surrogate mom in place and instead of his deceased wife. He found himself in court to answer for drug-related charges. Because of his financial clout and connections to the community, the Court was sympathetic to his plight, i.e. his wife's burning, that the Court ordered him to complete a drug diversion program, which would culminate in the dismissal of the charges when Teddy completed the program.

Algar was a different story. He recovered from his mom's passing. He seemed more strengthened by it. On one side, he should have had the sacred love of his mom preserved in a special place in his heart, and, on the other side, another more profane love, a Tigrana, that sort of bewitched him. But, Algar was no Edgar, a character far different than the opera. He was built to overpower his emotions with a disinterested sense of stoicism. The trigger on this particular characteristic may have been spawned by a father who was less loving and more compassionate about work, or a mother who cared more about the appearances of mothering but less about the intellectual needs of her child. In short, Algar could "game" the home life to his advantage. Rebecca DeBlaine was no threat. He had her under control. He knew how to manipulate her. At one family gathering, while he was seated on Rebecca's lap, he took her hand and placed it between his legs. Before she realized what had happened and removed her hand, the photographer snapped the picture, later giving it to the boy at his demand. Whenever she attempts to reprimand him for his behavior, he whisks out one of many copies of that picture to regain control. She needs the money desperately and, with Heiday's passing, she is assuming more responsibility over Algar.

Knowing this, one morning, he decides to test this control. He chooses a time when his father is being institutionalized by Court order. It is just DeBlaine and Algar in this large mansion. She serves him orange juice, which he deliberately drops off the table. DeBlaine does not see the spill but hears the cup crashing against the floor. She turns around and throws a towel at Algar, saying, "clean it up." Algar replies, "no. You clean it up." DeBlaine answers, "I will not." She then brings a second cup of orange juice and says, "don't spill this." Just as she turns her back, the second cup goes crashing to the floor spilling its contents onto the existing pool of orange juice. She is just about ready to slap Algar when the picture appears on the tabletop. She sees it and recoils. She places her hands to her face. Algar throws the towel into the face of DeBlaine, saying, "clean it up now." She tries to clean it in a standing position. Algar commands, "on hands and knees." DeBlaine gets on her hands and knees and begins cleaning the floor sobbing as she mops it up. He then shouts, "quit crying" pushing his foot against her rear.

Later, that day, another episode occurs and reeling from his first victory, Algar determines to further test his hypothesis of domination. DeBlaine appears more subservient to Algar and treats him real nice, saying, "I can make you a crepe suzette dessert or a chocolate brownie." Algar cavalierly demands, "chocolate brownie, no clothes." DeBlaine asks, "no clothes, what do you mean?" "You, no clothes," he repeats. "No, I cannot do. No," DeBlaine objects. Realizing the boy is holding the picture in the palm of his hand, she says, "I'll make it in the kitchen, no clothes, but you can't come in."

DeBlaine goes to the kitchen and locks the kitchen door. She worriedly strips off her clothes as the boy remains in the dining room of the home. She feels somewhat comforted by knowing that there is no way for the boy to see her in this condition because there are no interior windows to that kitchen. She begins making the chocolate brownies for Algar. Seemingly, more comfortable with making the brownies, she dances in the kitchen seeing her reflection against the stainless steel refrigeration unit. In the midst of the dance, the lights to the entire house go out and the emergency lights in designated spots go on. An alarm system chimes in raising the specter that a fire has broken out. Mindful of the last fire, just 2 years ago, DeBlaine goes into panic mode and races to unlock the kitchen door. She looks around and Algar is not seated at the dining room table and the front double doors are opened. Not knowing where the fire may be, DeBlaine scurries out the front door, naked and definitely concerned. When she exits the house, both front doors close and lock. In emergencies, the mansion utilizes a lockdown mode, which prevents entry with the usual common codes or keys.

Not seeing any fire and distressed as to where Algar is, she attempts to open the front doors but is unable to do so. She runs around the house trying to find Algar or an opening.

By the time she returns to the front of the house, the fire department arrives and DeBlaine attempts to cover herself up. The Fire Department comes to the home and the lights turn back on. Algar opens the front door and Battalion Chief Springer meets the boy again at the entrance. DeBlaine rushes into the house to get her clothes. Given her state of undress, DeBlaine never gets to tell her side of the story. Springer asks the boy what happened, Algar replies, "DeBlaine made brownies without clothes on." When DeBlaine finally returns to the front door, fully clothed, Springer asks, "were you making brownies for the boy with no clothes on?" DeBlaine just gasps, hesitating and not responding. Finally, she clamors out, "no or yes, I don't know." That response was taken as an admission of guilt. DeBlaine implores Springer, "don't put that in your report, please. Just say it was a false alarm." Springer leaves without making any further comment.

As the fire truck leaves the property, Algar smiles contently knowing that in the future DeBlaine is totally under his control.

CHAPTER EIGHT

Gizpaco's Tar Pits

The sun had sunk behind the distant horizon for some time now leaving the moon to bloom in its full glory. It's a harvest moon that creeps up from the horizon and ascends high into the bejeweled night sky. From a distance that yellowish orb seems to rest atop the old Trafalgar bridge – a bridge that carries only historical significance now since being replaced by a new-fangled one. Thus, it is seldom used. But this night is different. A silhouetted image of a tall lanky bent-over character, a galoot, happens over the bridge with the full crest of the moon as his backdrop. An hora of spilt gold traces over his body, as if gilded by the hand of Midas himself. He dons an old farmer's hat, black and battered from years of wear and punishing heat. His propulsive gait gives the appearance that if he leaned too far forward he would certainly fall off the bridge into the abyss below. His clothes are ragged and dirty. Parts of his flesh are exposed through the many holes that his garment no longer covers. His chin is pointed and so is his snout lodged on a pale long face.

He drags a canvas sack behind him, pulling it episodically as he waddles across the cobblestoned Trafalgar. There is a sound of clanging as his metal toed boots come into contact with the stones. On occasion, a spark rises from the metal abrading against the stones. He mumbles to himself in an unspoken language that only the morning vespers of a monk could understand. Whatever the cargo is in that sack, it has no choice but to go along with the stop and drag.

What is he doing and where is he going? As he begins his descent off the bridge, he makes an abrupt right turn and disappears into the darkness of overgrowth and shrubbery. The moonlight provides some light along the path he has chosen to walk. He strikes at the trees in a machete-like fashion with his right hand as his left hand firmly grasps the sack. He slowly makes his way to a pool, a waste pool of blackness that not even the moonlight can brighten. A black hole of nothingness that not even light can escape from. The pool is filled with spent oil, cooking grease, a natural-oozing tar, and braking fluids from businesses that choose an alternative to toxic waste disposal requirements.

Gizpaco is his name. He came from some place on the Iberian Peninsula but lay orphan as a stowaway on a transoceanic trip to the Americas. He was a throwaway baby with parents who had no other financial choice to keep the infant. They wanted a better life for him that they could not afford so they dropped him off in a puppy carrier on the docks near where an ocean liner was bound for Miami. He was not discovered by the crew until the third day in the voyage and, when inquiries went unanswered, the baby entered the country through Miami as the point of entry. He was never adopted but spent his formative years living in old Scottish church on the outskirts of Birmingham. At an early age he developed an interest in Greek Mythology and now fancies himself as Charon whose duty in life is to ferry the misguided to their proper place in the afterlife.

In the dead of this night, Gizpaco spins around 3-4 times with the sack whirling with him like a hammer thrower and he releases the sack which soars to a distant point into the pool and sinks into the ooze of petroleum hydrocarbon mixed with tar. Showing no reaction, Gizpaco disappears into the darkness.

CHAPTER NINE

One Billion Dollar Baby Knockout

Walking to the Board of County Commissioners' Meeting with his Assistant Chief Engineer Wade Terriff, Seve Aguado comments, "if I can bring this home for a little under a billion bucks our shore front homes and high rises will be saved." Wade adds, "in the long run, this is an ounce of prevention when we have the ability to plan." Seve further comments, "It's investing in our future. Do it while we can. There are many high rise buildings resting on a loose mixture of sand and mud and, although the developers core into the bedrock for stability, that rock is nothing more than limestone and oolite. To get to the real hard stuff, you got to drill down 3,000 to 4,000 feet." Wade notes, "these developers won't dig that deep, thereby endangering the lives of their inhabitants." As they march into the Commissioners' Conference Room, Seve whispers to Wade, "sell, sell, sell."

Chairman Douglas Jackson calls the meeting to order. "Our first matter on the agenda and one that is most important is the Proposed Arc of Tranquility project. We have circulated the report of our Chief Engineer to our fellow Commissioners for comment. It is now open for questions. Commissioner Enright from District 13 who has posted some questions, you may proceed." Monte Enright answers, "thank you, Chairman."

Monte Enright was born and raised in South Florida choosing to skip college after high school and pioneer a start-up dredging business that yielded spectacular profits over the years. He is of medium build in his late 50's and had to work very hard to get to this position in life. His business has grown to an 80-man team operating in many of the lower counties of South Florida. He owns several homes with one located in District 13 and the others situated in other states. He has desires to accede to high political position. He is irritated by Seve, his intelligence, his academic background, his youth, and, especially, his good looks. He worries that Seve's popularity with the Commissioners and other government workers and higher-ups makes him the candidate of choice for Mayor or, even, Governor. This major project could send Seve into the ionosphere of influence and clout that will seal his chances at future elected office.

Enright: "Good evening, Mr. Aguado. You state in your report that the Arc of Tranquility will cost approximately $37,000 per linear yard of artificial reef breakwater for the estimated 12 to 13-mile stretch between the breakwater of the Port of Miami and the County line just north of Golden Beach. You estimate the cost of the reef to run just under One Billion Dollars, is that right?"

Aguado: "Yes, that's right."

Enright: "You plan on paying for it through State and Federal subsidies, County funds, bond measures, and automotive licensing fees and gas taxes."

Aguado: "Yes, those are the projections."

Enright: "I have one simple question – 'Why?' Why should be commit the funds to this ridiculous project when there is no evidence of massive flooding anywhere in the County?"

Aguado: "It's better to plan ahead than to wait for misfortune to arrive."

Enright: "I understand that concept but what is more troubling are the statistics you arrive at to justify this expensive project. Even, with the best evidence from the NOAA, water levels have risen to only 2 feet over the last 20 years. Our condominiums and high-rise buildings have not been threatened to the point they need immediate escarpments somewhere in the middle of the Atlantic Ocean as you propose."

Aguado: "Commissioner Enright, there is no evidence that the water levels are subsiding. All reports from the State of Florida and the Federal government prove that it is only a matter of time before flooding becomes a 'red hot button' issue."

Enright: "Even if some of your statistical data has some credible worthiness, how does that affect the many landlocked districts of the County that don't feel they should save the waterfront districts from this peril?"

Aguado: "Because tourist dollars don't discriminate when coming to Miami and Miami Beach. We should operate with unanimity."

Enright: "Why should residents and constituents of my District and other landlocked districts pony up more in gas taxes and car registration fees to protect those waterfront Districts that generate more revenue from bed taxes and inflated land values? Let them pay for their planning deficiencies. They have the money."

Aguado: "Because it is the right thing to do. We work and operate as a County to protect all the members and residents of our County."

Enright: "Isn't it true you came up with this wild idea so you could tout yourself as a visionary worthy of higher political office?"

Aguado: "No. I did it as my obligation as a Chief Engineer; not as a candidate."

Enright: "I'll tell you this, I'll be damned if I will vote for this project. It's not the time or the place for it. You offer no guarantees that even if the reef breakwater is placed some two miles offshore that will remedy global warming and rising floodwaters. It is preposterous to even consider this "mickey mouse" project."

After some additional discussions, the Commissioners voted down the proposed Arc of Tranquility with 5 waterfront Districts voting for it and 8 landlocked Districts voting against it.

With the votes casts, Aguado was fuming. His power base was weakened and it was the first time in his life that someone challenged him to the point of humiliating him. His stature at the County had been toppled off of its pedestal. And he was mad.

CHAPTER TEN

Dredging Bones

A call comes into the home of Monte Enright. The home is a palatial wonder. Marble adorning walls and walkways. Paintings during the Impressionist Period on display, larger than life, consume the entire walls of the residence. From his first job as a teenager dredging a pool filled with silt and other muddy sediment caused by a hurricane, he saw the opportunity a dredging concern could unearth; revenue from extracting water in places they should not be and carving out terrain where water should be. His early revenues funded larger dredgers and from larger dredgers he contracted larger projects. One such major project was the intracoastal waterway. As the population began to swell, there was more need for boats. Marinas had to be built to house the boats. With surging demand and wealth accretion, boat owners became yacht and ship owners. Each one trying to outdo the next in having the prized ship of the fleet. Capitalism fed off this competition and larger ships needed larger marinas and the inland passageways to the sea had to be deepened and widened. Enright Way Dredging (EWD) went along for the ride and the profits it netted were enormous. EWD has developed into one of the largest dredgers in South Florida.

Monte answers the call. "What's Up?" with a characteristic upbeat sound. "This is Manny," the EWD's field superintendent on a back bay project on the west end of Pembroke Pines. Manny tells Monte, "some guy came up to me inquiring into buying a dredging rig. He says, he knows you." Monte asks, "what's his name?" "Some guy name Peter, that's all he said," answers

Manny. "I don't know a Peter, but who knows I could have run into him when I was running for Commissioner." Monte hesitates for a moment, ruminating, then states, "tell him I'll see him at the site after the workday's done, closer to early evening." Manny responds, "Okay, boss."

Later that day, toward early evening, Monte stands next to a motorboat that is on the shore of the bay. Some new developments are going in and Monte spies them waiting for the potential customer to arrive. His rig sits on the water in the center of the bay. He decides to call Manny about the condition of the rig. "Hello, Manny, this is Monte. How come the rig looks beat up? The lettering on the side is so faded one cannot see the name "Enright." Manny stutters a bit, "I was going to bring it up to you, but I wanted to get further along in the project." Monte replies, "what does the lettering on the side of the rig have to do with the project? It's my company and I need to advertise anyway I can to keep up with my competitors. Next Saturday have someone come out and repaint the lettering please." Manny answers, "okay, Boss." Somewhat displeased with the sight and the call, Monte makes a disgusted face, but sees a man approach and commences to smile. "You are Peter?" "Yes," says the man. The man looks to be Russian, tan and well built. "I guess you don't look like a Peter," says Monte chuckling. "Call me Pedro," the man responds laughing. "There you go," says Monte. He then says, "have we met before?" "Yes, when you ran for office," Peter says. "I shook a lot of hands and knocked on a lot of doors so I apologize if I don't remember who you are," mentions Monte. Looking out at the rig on the water, pointing to it, "there she be. She's a beauty. Needs a little painting, but, boy, can she dredge. See the red cutter's edge." "Yes," says Peter. "That will cut away at clay, limestone and other dirt like a burning knife through butter," notes Monte. "Any way we can see it?" inquires Peter. "Sure, that's why the boat's here. You want to step in. Don't get your trousers wet." Before getting into the boat, two other men appear walking close to the boat. "Do you mind if I bring a couple of my investors along for the tour?" says Peter. Looking around, in this deserted place where skeletons of structures are coming into shape, Monte sizes up the situation and, with some hesitation, then says, "I think we can get 4 into this boat."

After departing the shore, Monte asks the two gentlemen their names but there is no response. They seem serious but Peter injects, "they are recently here from Russia. They don't speak English or, for that matter, Spanish."

The boat arrives at the rig and the men step off.

Monte takes the men into the control room. "Here is where it all happens," states Monte showing them the gauges, buttons, and operating switches on the main pad. Peter asks, "how do you operate the cutter?" "Go to the main pad and press this cutter switch simultaneously punching this switch on the arm, which raises and lowers the arm into the water. While dredging, the sediment and other debris are sucked up and transported through a pipeline to an open field, where they are physically removed by disposal trucks," pointing to the pipeline that runs across the waterway to an empty lot.

Peter says, "Can I try?" "Sure," says Monte. Speaking out loud, "okay, I push this button to rise and lower the arm into the water and simultaneously press the button for the cutter to work." The arm lowers into the water. Monte adds, "now, let the arm reach the bottom before hitting the cutter switch." Peter comments, "I see." While both men are fixated on the screen, the two identified men grab the arms of Monte restraining him from striking back. They bind his hands with zip ties and he attempts to kick the men, but one gives him a swift kick to the groin that causes him to bend over. While his back is turned, Peter gags Monte saying, "we want this to be as quiet as possible." The struggle ensues with Monte trying to fight any way he can, kicking and shoving, but the three men overpower him and they zip tie his legs together. Other than some wrangling, they lift up

Monte and take him to the outside edge of the control room.

Peter says to the other Russian, Grigori, "let's see how he swims." They hurl Monte into the muddy waters, where, on his back, he tries to float to prevent from sinking into the bay water. While the other two men watch outside at the spectacle of Monte fighting for his life, they calmly smile and occasionally laugh to themselves. In the meantime, Peter has returned to the control room and raises the arm off the bottom of the bay floor. As it rises to the surface, he positions the arm toward the wading Monte. Monte sees the arm rising out of the water like some primeval monster and then sees the grooved cutter in bright red rise also above the water line. Monte helplessly shakes his head from side to side, looking up at the two Russians. They smile. Peter fires up the cutter and lowers the arm and cutter directly onto Monte, cutting him into a million pieces. The pieces are sucked up into the pipeline and deposited onto the vacant lot.

The men return in the motorboat and trek over to the vacant lot. "It's like a cremation by water. It's hard to determine if these are chicken bones from dog bones." The men fully satisfied with the operation leave the area.

CHAPTER ELEVEN

Seductive Overtures

When she walked in, she knew she had the job. She was a perfect fit. She had the poise, personality, confidence and intelligence to win the hearts of the two interviewers – both women. She graduated from Dartmouth College in New Hampshire and obtained a Master's degree from Stanford and a Ph.d from Harvard. All degrees were in Economics. She was the Heisman trophy winner for Economics. She was sought after and offered many opportunities for these academic pursuits. But she was choosy and she had her reasons why, but she kept them to herself. Lofty goals were hers to obtain and no one, but no one, was going to get in her way.

As one of the largest economic firms in the country, Tyesha Biggerstaff knew from the moment she walked in, she was the candidate of choice, the heir apparent to the sought after position as Junior Economic Consultant – Worldwide Investments of McElroy Management. She thinks to herself this is her stage debut; the new nova in the field of Economics has come to assume the throne in this belfry of economic preeminence.

This is no ordinary job interview. This is one in which the firm's two top economists are inquiring as to Tyesha's qualifications. They hunger for the best. If they don't choose the best, then that person may work for their competition. To be on top, they need the best minds working for them; not working against them.

One interviewer is Meghan Middlebrook. She is in her mid 40's with a quick wit and vibrant sense of humor. But she is a math whiz and it would take a very gifted mind to pull something over on her. She doesn't miss a nuance or any subtext. Middlebrook achieved her level of competence from her skills passed down from generations of mathematicians who went on to prestigious East Coast universities. She had no gene shaping that framed her talent. It was just simply God-given talent. Meghan is married to Vinnie Fratellino and happily married for 22 years. She has had difficulties getting pregnant and, even with creative measures of IVF, those did not do the trick. Vinnie is 5 years younger than Meghan and has brought into their relationship a child he fathered when he was 18 years old. The child is named Meredith and she just turned 23 years. Meredith and Meghan do not get along, primarily, because Meredith's mom is so active in her life. Her mom has filled her head with notions that hadn't Meghan forced herself upon Vinnie, Meredith would have had a full Italian household with merriment, wine and Italian song. She resents Meghan in so many ways but puts up with a lot of things just to please her dad.

The other interviewer is Prosperity Glendale. In her early 50's, she is more set in doing things in a calibrated, orderly way. She likes formulas, equations, and mathematical expressions. In her early childhood, her parents thought that her behavior was a little anti-social and disconnected. She was a good student but got irritated in class when students would not sit in their assigned seats. She felt that there was an order to that assignment and to break that order would result in disruption or chaos. In 5th grade this became all too apparent, when Prosperity could not sleep at night bemoaning the change in seat assignments. Thinking that there was something more medically involved with this type of behavior and sensing this may be a sign of autism, they had their daughter undergo a brain scan. The scan came back that Prosperity had the "ring of fire" syndrome, which caught early could be treated by medication. The medication proved to be more damaging to the child by creating an emotional roller-coaster that she would withstand, such as sleepless nights, suicidal ideations, and mid-day fatigue. They thought she might be better off without medication. Once off the medication, her focus returned and she excelled in math incredibly well, working as the youngest teacher's assistant at the University of Pennsylvania at the age of 17 years. After some time, the parents thought they missed the boat and went to a geneticist to inquire if they should have had Prosperity genetically shaped. They also went to see if it wasn't too late, could they indulge stem cell therapy to remedy the "ring of fire" disorder. The conclusion of the geneticist at that time was that it was too late. Prosperity has never had any kind of relationship with a woman or man. She seems disinterested in sex or gender preferences. If it weren't for math and economic statistics, she would be lost in a world without any compass heading; nothing to fall back onto. But, at McElroy, she is an important cog in the apparatus. She looks upon her job as her life and that her personal life is not existent to trivial. She believes that her personal life "is an unnecessary interruption of her career." Her attire has won her the name in the office as the "drab dresser."

Meghan opens the interview by saying: "Welcome, Tyesha, to McElroy. Please have a seat." Tyesha is an African American mix with some traces of French background having blue eyes and a great figure. She is 24 1/2 years old. She wears a black dress with a hemline 3-4 inches above the knee. She is wearing pantyhose and a red scarf around her neck. Black heels with reddish hue make a nice presentation for the interviewers. She thinks to herself, "I know what they want. They want me." She seductively descends to her seat as Meghan watches slowly. Before Meghan can continue, Tyesha suggests, "before I do any interview, I'd like to meditate for a moment or so to get a spiritual feeling of the atmosphere of the room." Meghan replies, "if that is your preference, please do so. We don't wish to tread on anything that might be religious."

Tyesha closes her eyes and thinks to herself, "remember, what you were taught in autonomous sensory meridian response (ASMR) class -- let them feel calm and then you can control." Tyesha whispers ever so softly, "could we have complete quiet? Quiet makes us calm and relaxed." Tyesha crosses her legs and rubs her nylons making a sound that gently breaks the cold silence of the room. She breathe slowly asking Meghan and Prosperity to join in. In whispered tones, "breathe in and breathe out," blowing as she recites it over and over. She rubs her nylons again saying "caress" in such dulcet tones. She uncrosses her legs and continues to glide her hands up and down her legs making a long soft textured sound. She pulls out a piece of paper from her pocket making a crinkling sound. She writes on the paper and then another paper and crumples both up and hands the crumpled paper to each Interviewer. Both open the crumpled papers and Prosperity puts a hand to her mouth when she reads, "I love you." Meghan is not so seduced and crumples the paper back up and says, "is the meditation over?" "Almost," says Tyesha. She gets up and holds out her hands to both Meghan and Prosperity. Prosperity willingly extends her hand and grasps Tyesha's hand. Meghan, a little more hesitant, but seeing Prosperity engage so willingly, extends her hand to Tyesha, who grabs it making a three-way connection and announces, "this is our ring of fire." Through some pre-meeting inquiry, Tyesha had learned of Prosperity's medical condition and had utilized it to gain access to Prosperity. Prosperity blushes at the remark and appears to be captivated by Tyesha. After the hand holding, Tyesha bends over and kisses Prosperity's hand. Again, this triggers Prosperity to blush. Meghan then announces, "let's get back to the reason why we are here -- To determine your qualifications for the Junior Economic Consultant job."

Meghan continues, "We have looked at your resume, spoken to your headhunter, reviewed transcripts of your grades at some of the most prestigious universities in this country and contacted a few of your personal references." We would like to know your take on the "Principle of Increasing Opportunity Cost." Tyesha answers, "it is a principle that as one increases the production of one good, the opportunity cost of producing that next unit increases." Meghan asks, "do you agree with that principle or do you believe it is no longer relevant in the workplace?" "Yes," says Tyesha, "it is still relevant. For example, if you'd put $1,000 in the bank, you would only realize a few pennies of interest in the long term. If you put that $1,000 into a piece of real property, one would realize an 8% to 12% cap. rate per annum on that return; but, if you put that $1,000 into high risk venture green business or genetics, one could realize a 1,000% per annum on that money. Thus, the principle is viable today as it was when it was propounded years ago." "Nice answer," says Meghan.

Still rubbing her legs, Meghan takes notice. Tyesha goes on by asserting, "that principle is at play here. If I have a certain value to a food company as an employee, that value would be far less than my value at an economics firm. If I did work for the food company, my value would be far less than my opportunity value. But from the Nash equilibrium, if each player knows the equilibrium strategies of the other players and there is nothing to gain by changing their strategy, then the result is predictable. If my strategy is to win the interview and your strategy is to hire the best employee, and we don't change those strategies, then the result can be predicted to an absolute certainty."

Meghan, a little heady, states: "What do you predict the outcome of this interview is?" Tyesha says, as she slightly spreads her legs, "that's completely up to you." Meghan looks closely, somewhat mesmerized by Tyesha and the legs crossing and rubbing and smiles at Tyesha. Tyesha smiles back. "We'll have an answer for you in the next day. You don't have to hold your breath, just whisper breathing in and out that you most probably will get the job," says Meghan. Tyesha says, "thank you," smothering a laugh.

CHAPTER TWELVE

Massaging the Message

One thing the Pridleys enjoyed in their twilight years was a deep and soothing massage at Mid-Apple Massage. Jan Pridley wasn't walking as well when she was in her 70's and her physician had recommended physical therapy to prevent atrophy from creeping up and in. She had tried physical therapy but it was a little less holistic and more mechanical for her personal tastes. Her husband of 45 years knew that her confinement to a wheelchair could never be the answer. In his opinion it was the quickest way to die. Glen Pridley had a passion for keeping physically fit and the mirrors around the house are evident proof of his feelings and looking good. For a man in his early 80's he was in tip top shape. Jan would comment when he would pose in front of any mirror and flex, "you're a narcissist," with a warm engaging laugh. She was very proud that he tried to maintain his youthful appearance rather than surrendering to the eroding ravages of age. He wasn't about himself in a selfish sense but he cared for her in such a close and passionate way. He never cheated on her and was the loyal pup that would wait outside the salon during her hair appointments.

There was a time in which they would walk to Mid-Apple Massage but Jan's arthritic condition has limited her walking to home. They occasionally go to restaurants and very infrequently to church, but it is the weekly massage they both enjoy. A moment for a relaxed stroking of the flesh that eases the tensions brought on with the physical demands of the day. The couple enjoyed the camaraderie of Chessy, an older masseur, who worked there. He had a warm sense of humor and and a "golden touch" to his therapy that they relished. When they heard he was undergoing chemotherapy they were quite a bit saddened and his appearance changed. He survived the cancer scare but determined to move out of the Manhattan area and head to the warmer climes of Surprise, Arizona. This is the first time they have returned to Mid-Apple since his departure. They wonder if the new masseur would be just as good.

They both amble into the massage parlor and sit down. They wait for a few moments and then Sabrina comes in. "Hi," she says, "I'm Sabrina Zablowsky, and I'm your assigned masseuse. Come follow me." She is none other than the girl that beat up Daryl Craver. She hasn't changed the platinum blonde hair but her mannerisms are less austere. She is friendly. She sports a nice green short dress. As Jan hobbles along, Sabrina says, "watch your step here. We go down three steps." A little ornery, Jan quips, "I've been here many times. I know these steps." Sabrina cavalierly retorts, "we know you have and we appreciate your business. Thank you for coming." That cools Jan's temperament a bit. Jan is not upset with Sabrina personally; she is upset to where this station in her life has brought her. She has difficulty walking and the stigmata of time has made its unruly imprint all over her scourged body. Rather than to politely tell Sabrina she is beautiful, it is far better to leave that unsaid because it would only then refocus the attention back to Sabrina.

"Since you know the drill, here are the changing rooms. Come out with towels on and lay face down on the massage tables. I will return shortly with the oils and other lubricants," Sabrina says in a soothing voice.

In adjacent changing rooms, Jan whispers to Glen, "why did we have to get her. She's a tramp." Glen replies, "you don't know that; you're guessing. She seems to know her way around a massage salon." Jan continues, "she sashays in here likes she's a Egyptian princess. She works for us now." Glen corrects Jan, "she works ON us. You know how you feel after a massage. Let her be." Jan's anger passes and they both come out toweled and lie face down on their respective massage tables not more than one foot apart. While they wait, Jan holds out her hand and Glen grasps it, saying "I love you." Glen echoes, "I love you too."

Sabrina returns wearing a white medical coat over her green dress to assure that none of the oils and lubricants get on her dress. She goes over to the couple and states, "are you ready for a fulfilling warm and fragrance-filled massage?" Both nod their heads with Glen managing to say, "yes." "Good," says Sabrina, "I will be applying a denatured balm that penetrates the skin and muscle tissue. It's a new extract being used in the massage industry." The couple listen intently as she applies the balm to the back of the necks of Jan and Glen. She sings a little Russian song that aids the massage effect that harmonizes with the pleasant sounds of water gushing over a brook that plays repeatedly in the background. The massage seems to be working and Sabrina smiles. She knows that the balm is laden with anesthetic properties that have characteristics similar to gamma-hydroxybutyric acid, a central nervous system depressant. As she rubs it deep into the tissues of Jan and Glen's neck and back, they both are placed in a twilight state of semi-consciousness unaware of their surroundings or experiences. After a few minutes pass, Sabrina unclasps the holding hands of the couple and the arms fall to the side of the massage tables. She lowers the towel on Jan's back making sure the towel does not expose Jan's buttocks and commences to massage her back thoroughly applying oils and other balms to her back. Sabrina has learned over the years that while in a deep trance massage (a DTM), the person undergoing a massage can hear clearly. Sabrina gets up close to Jan's right ear and whispers, "you believe this is the best massage you ever felt. When you awake, you will be totally satisfied and happy that I massaged you. You will feel an innermost closeness to me like you never felt with anyone at any time." She repeats these lines over and over again as she massages Jan's neck, legs and arms. Minutes pass as she maneuvers around the table that Jan lies. Sabrina thinks more darkly that she can cast a spell on Jan to change her emotionally. This sinister thought overwhelms her mind uncontrollably and finally has no other exit than for her to utter, "when you awake, you will look upon me as your shaman that gives you purpose and direction. You will trust my advice to you." She walks to the other side of the table, as if her words are anointing Jan's mind and body with precious incense and sacred unguent, saying, "You trust me as your shaman and, obligingly, listen to everything I say."

She then goes to Glen. She applies more denatured balm to his neck to insure he is still under the full anesthetic of the balm. Though he is in a state of unconsciousness, she tells him, "turn over honey, I need to do the other side." He seems to understand and Sabrina helps him to turn over. Once he turns over facing up, he falls back into this state of sleepiness. She whispers in his ear so Jan cannot hear her words, "you really like me and what I am doing. You want to come here and see me often, even if it is alone. You love my massages and think I am beautiful." She repeats these lines as she massages his chest, arms and legs. Then, she goes to his feet and kneads them. Sabrina ponders how can she get him to help her financially. She knows from their financial statements, he is worth millions and gets a healthy monthly annuity from an insurance company. The age difference is unimportant. The objective is the ends justify the means. She provides the subtle hypnotic suggestion when she mutters, "you are attracted to me and desire me. No matter who is present, you want to show you crave me. You don't care. You want to touch me, hold me, kiss me." After saying these remarks at the same time, she massages his face with her smooth hands, she plants a kiss on his lips. She sees no reaction. Then she kisses again sustaining it a little longer. She notices a slight movement of his upper lip. She again recites, "you want to touch me, hold me, kiss me. Kiss me real hard." Sabrina goes in for a deeper kiss this time and, for the first time, Glen kisses back. Sabrina responds, "see, how wonderful and easy that is?" She goes back down on Glen's lips and French kisses him. Glen unaware of what is going on somehow reciprocates on auto-pilot by sticking his tongue into Sabrina's mouth. Sabrina laughs with enthusiasm. Still whispering into his ear, "you are a good kisser. We'll do that again soon. Wasn't that fun?" As she looks over to Jan. Jan is deep in sleep face down and unmindful of what lechery has occurred.

Anxious to see the reaction of the DTM in conjunction with the effects of the denatured balm and hypnotic suggestion, Sabrina waits a full 40 minutes before the two come to their senses.

The first reaction caught Sabrina completely by surprise. Jan stretches out her arms like she just had awaken from a long slumber, looking over at Sabrina with a broad smile. "I feel great. I haven't felt like this in years." She gets off the table and the towel falls to the floor. "You did a great job. What's your name again?" asks Jan. "Sabrina," she says, "maybe you should put that towel back on to cover yourself." Jan replies, "oh, yes. Thank you for noticing. I don't want to attract too much attention," laughing in the direction of Sabrina. She adds, "I feel rejuvenated like I could dance all night," moving around in a circle. Sabrina thinks to herself, "what happened? Did I change her behavior or reboot her memory banks? Whatever it is, she apparently likes me." She hesitates and ponders for a moment, "does she trust me? How do I test that now?" Sabrina worries that this could be the defining point in which her treachery is revealed to the Pridleys. She does the unthinkable and blurts out, "we are having some trouble processing your payment for the massage. Do you have any hesitations about us holding your wedding ring until we are able to complete that process?" Barely finishing her remarks, Jan hands over her wedding ring to Sabrina, saying,

"I trust you with this." Sabrina's uncontrollable excitement over this turn of events causes her to laugh hysterically, but her sense of decency has gotten the better of her and she says, "it was just a thought. This is a cherished possession. You should have it." She hands the ring back. She does add, "before your husband wakes up, could you do me a favor? Next time, you come in, could you wear a green and white dress with white nylons?" Jan smiles, "I don't see why not," laughing as well. "I want to look my best when I come here," she adds. She holds out her hand to Sabrina and Sabrina grabs it for a moment and then lets go.

Glen begins to come out of his sleepy state. Sabrina wonders what will be Glen's response to all this? Maybe he heard the dialogue between Jan and her and is mad that she is preying upon this older innocent couple. She thinks if he was aware of the kissing, he's not going to make that admission of guilt in the presence of Jan because he was a reciprocal participant in the exercise. But he could also accuse her of attempting to drug him to do things against his will. Jan has not revealed anything that would establish that she was aware of the kissing and, certainly, would have been offended and would have said something immediately after waking. But she didn't. Now, the reaction for Glen is forthcoming. It appears first with a pleasant smile on his face and he rubs his lips a little. Sabrina looks on for any clues as to his demeanor. Then, he lets out a big sigh and says, "I just had the greatest dream of all time. I felt so happy, in love, and my body is tingling from the massage." He looks at Sabrina, "thank you for the best massage I have ever had. You are such a sweet girl." In the presence of his listening wife, "you are such an attractive, beautiful woman." After 45 years of marriage, that remark should have crossed the lines of diplomacy as an act of bold, outright flirtation, stoking the fires of discontent given the pre-massage disposition of Jan. But, after the massage, Jan was radiantly happy and joins, "she is an attractive woman and I want to see her again." Then, Glen follows, "we would like to see you again." Sabrina winks at Glen, which Jan notices, and she winks back at Sabrina and laughs.

As they leave the salon, Sabrina smiles and delicately plans her next attack.

CHAPTER THIRTEEN

Profiling

Portland's District Attorney Harry Berger has developed a good sense of profiling having himself at one time worked for the Sheriff's Department in their CSI Department. Choosing to raise the bar, he studied at night at law school and obtained his JD. Once he passed the bar, he had enough connections and clout to work for the District Attorney's offices as an upstart attorney. He prosecuted many drug and white collar crime cases and developed a good rapport with the sitting judges. With the backing of the Sheriff's Department and local support from Judges and the bar, he won an election to District Attorney. He has done a good job in that regard and has fended off challenges over the years for that position.

He looks at a white collar investigation report regarding organized crime compiled by the FBI local offices in Portland, Oregon. There has been an uptick in white collar internet crimes that he expected would be on the rise. He looks at the mug shots of the suspects and defendants in those criminal cases and noted one peculiar similarity -- all were good-looking.

He calls the Bureau's Chief, Sam Ideman, and inquires about that similarity. "Hi, Sam. I read your report." Sam says, "whatcha think of it?" "It's good but did you notice something when you looked at the mug shots?" says Harry. "No. They were all ugly," stammers Sam. "No. The opposite – they were all good-looking. Is that coincidence or is there a rhyme or reason for it?" says Harry. Sam, somewhat taken aback by his remarks, says, "are you insinuating that we only prosecute ugly looking people at the federal level?" "No. I'm not insinuating anything. I just noticed that they were all good-looking," remarks Harry. "It's just coincidence. Nothing more than coincidence," responds Sam. He adds, "we went through a period of uglies; now, lovelies are in vogue." Harry counters, "when was the last time lovelies were in vogue?" Sam answers, "frankly, never." "I'm going to watch this closely," concludes Harry.

CHAPTER FOURTEEN

Graphene Oxide Fiends

They were students at the University of Texas and believed, innocently, that they had stumbled onto the next revolutionary idea in self-charging batteries. They thought by nudging graphene oxide out of popularity and replacing it with silica oxide or dioxide, namely, sand, the world could run on their batteries with an inexhaustible supply of that element. These students reasoned that graphene oxide has harmful effects on immune cell activation and that toxic chemicals have to be used at high temperatures to grow graphene. Because of those considerations, they believed it was more green-worthy to work with sand where an abundance of it surrounds the globe.

Dirk Rainjoy, a 22-year old graduate student in the Engineering Department, has been studying self-charging batteries for quite some time. He believes that battery usage will keep down the carbon footprint and reduce harmful greenhouse gases, such as methane and carbon dioxide. He studied the componentry of silica oxide and compared it with graphene oxide. The primary difference between the two – graphene was not naturally occurring on earth and had to be grown in unrealistic and disturbing conditions. The graphene is rolled out on sheets and consists of some toxic qualities and impurities. He joined forces with another innovator, Picard Dodieaux, who has a chemical engineering degree from that institution. Both were gifted students, who excelled in their academic pursuits and achieved considerable recognition before their scholarly work. Both had picture-perfect good looks to bat.

When they launched Sand Sinergy, they thought they had arrived. But there was more instore for them than they could have ever anticipated.

They produced a self-charging battery that could self-charge solely based upon moisture in the air and its interaction with sand. The competition heard about it and wanted to square off against it. This was business and this new sand technology could paralyze their business – it could put them out of business. Self-Charge International (SCI) approaches Picard and asks how the system works and is interested in acquiring a stock interest in the company. Picard asks, "Who am I speaking with?" The voice on the other end states, "Jules. I'm a student from Northern Arizona University and I'm doing a research paper on this new technology." Picard smartly answers, "Jules, this technology is still in development and we have not protected its proprietary process at the moment. We cannot supply any information until development is complete." "Is there a way I can tour your facility?" asks Jules. Picard replies, "No, that won't be possible. The place is in disarray." Jules comments, "Give me a call when the development is achieved." "Certainly," says Picard.

Picard was also doubly concerned that the technology has not been engineered to his liking. He has been assigned to quality control and research. He was having dark disturbing doubts about getting a prototype for showcasing. Some of the investors were "hoodwinked" into believing that sand was a good and natural alternative to graphene. Picard now worries, "what will the investors do if we can't deliver a working product soon? Will they sue and all I will see from this is a mountain of legal paperwork and no profit? Will I have to file bankruptcy to keep them away from what little assets I have?" These worries overwhelm him and he reaches out to his friend in need, his compatriot in this venture, Dirk. "Hi, Dirk, this is Picard." "Hi," is Dirk's response. He continues sensing a strained pause in Picard's voice, "is everything alright?" Picard pours out his soul,

"Are we doing the right thing? I just had a strange call from allegedly a student from a University asking about our process, but I didn't tell him." "Be patient," says Dirk, "we are closing in on it. The sensors have to be fine-tuned at a microscopic level to collect the slightest trace of moisture for it to work." "Some of the investors have groused that there are cost overruns and we are 6 months behind on our production schedule," frets Picard. "Once our product is in place, we will make everyone a believer," confidently Dirk states.

Dirk has always been the leader. He exudes positivity, a penchant to make things happen. When he was an undergrad at Texas U, he charmed his way to success with a battery configuration that stumped the Engineering Department. He received high accolades for the feat but he wasn't opposed to getting down and dirty to get to where he wanted to go. The night before the presentation he wanted to ensure his chances for success so he flirted with one of the Engineering Professors. The evening ended with a sexual encounter and, as fate would have it, that Professor gave him flying colors at his night's performance and later at the presentation.

Dirk was unconcerned about Picard's worrisome nature. He thinks, "there are so many other plays we can make even if the project is an absolute failure. We can sell whatever state our work-in-progress is to another competitor, who will then "deep-six" it into nonexistence. We can take on more investors and tweak the technology into another direction. We can sell it off into Non-Fungible Tokens (NFTs). We can sell the company at bargain basement price and exit the field altogether." What concerned Dirk more than anything else, "what happens if it is a success? We would be numero uno, the king of self-charging. But, suddenly, the tiger is now on our backs to deliver. Thousands of components would have to be shipped everywhere. We would be going from 10 miles an hour to 1,500 miles an hour. It would be enormous pressure to meet the needs of the companies involved as well as the general public." Dirk then looks at the other side, a side that is not characteristically is his to own, "companies around the globe would be fixated on improving our technology, simplifying it and moving the industry in another direction. What this means is we would have an influx of cash for the short term, as the sharks would eat away at our corpus until we were totally annihilated."

The next day, Picard receives a letter from an attorney representing SCI. The letter states:

> "Please be advised that our firm has been retained to represent SCI in a potential patent infringement action against your company Sand Sinergy. It is our belief that your silica oxide process has infringed on the graphene process developed and patented by SCI. We would ask that you 'cease and desist' all further development of this process or we will seek the court's intervention in this matter for the issuance of temporary restraining orders and preliminary and permanent injunctions."

When he reads the letter, he drops it to the floor in shock. He imagines to himself that his business is being shuttered and people are laughing at him for his failure to bring the product to market. Looking around as if an answer lies on the table he sits at, he contemplates, "maybe I should relinquish my interest in Sand Sinergy. I have received so little from it at this point, it almost seems ludicrous not to." He takes a deep breath, sighs for a moment and calls Dirk. "We are going to be sued if we continue with the sand tech." Dirk asks, "why?" Picard retorts, "this attorney says he's going to sue us if we don't cease and desist." Dirk counters, "he's delusional. We have the right to bring new technology to the marketplace." Picard adds, "he says, it's patent infringement." Dirk effortlessly answers laughing, "we haven't infringed on any patents. He's nuts. Send the letter to our attorneys for reply. Don't waste another moment on this inanity."

However, some reality set in when Dirk reads the letter on his own. Further down in the article, mention is made to the sensors that absorb ambient moisture for the self-charging to work. Those sensors were developed, fabricated and separately patented by SCI. Now, Dirk can read the tea leaves with absolute clarity. SCI has a legal position over those sensors when it doesn't have it over the sand. Nevertheless, SCI would be able to prevail on its claims. To confirm his suspicions, Dirk contacts Paul Locke, a patent specialist out of Chicago, who confirms that SCI would prevail on the sensor claims.

That call was the most upsetting conversation Dirk has ever had in his life. Sand Sinergy's budget didn't call for sensor development and his investors are not going to fund something like that. If he fights the lawsuit, money for development will be wasted on legal fees that he won't recover at the end of the suit. If he procures new investors to build the new sensors, he will spend maybe one to two years in R&D to bear fruit. In the meantime, current investors, who hear of the existence of the potential lawsuit, will not be sympathetic to Dirk or Picard in their failure to explain this in the first place that the sensors were developed by another company. They would hold the two men accountable for misrepresentation. They would never have invested in a lawsuit in the first place.

Like having sex with a Professor before his presentation, Dirk plans a counterattack against SCI.

He goes to a couple of his friends at Texas U working in the Health Department and ask them to conduct a test on the safety of pocket size graphene self-charging batteries for cell phones. "Steve," says Dirk, "hi. It's been a long time. Could you do me a favor and conduct some safety and health tests on the graphene self-charging units for inhalation purposes? I'll send over some funds for testing."

Months later, a report surfaces that regular contact with

graphene oxide should be avoided but shows low toxicity.

Through a newspaper publication, it is announced that there is a level of toxicity associated with regular use of graphene failing to incorporate portions of the study. SCI heard of and ultimately reads the article and believes that Dirk and Picard are behind it. SCI files a claim of libel and defamation against the newspaper and Dirk and Picard. As the lawsuit rages on, Dirk sees his ideas behind the sand technology beginning to dry up along with venture capital. Cornered he determines to take swift action. Dirk decides that a criminal response is the appropriate response. One day, he takes dynamite and places it around SCI's warehouse, blowing it up. It didn't take long before law enforcement saw camera footage of a man wearing a creepy crawler outfit placing the dynamite around the premises to know it was Dirk.

Dirk was arrested. The newspaper retracted the article about toxicity of graphene. The criminal case got front page attention on a national level. "Ft. Worth Engineer arrested for blowing up competitor's building." Harry Berger reads that article and comments to himself, "another good looking man bites the dust."

CHAPTER FIFTEEN

DeBlaine's Contained

Algar's seventh birthday appeared and went with Algar exhibiting disappointment with the cake. Algar's dad was still in a place for the mentally distressed but now placed in a locked ward because he had developed signs of schizophrenia, which they hope in the long run is treatable. His businesses are run by adept individuals and Rebecca receives her monthly allowance from them which has increased with Theodore's absence from the residence.

"I wanted devil's food cake with chocolate frosting," he dictates. Rebecca grabs the cake and begins to walk away, saying, "I'm heartily sorry, my apologies." He grabs a piece of the cake while she retrieves the cake and the cake pad not noticing the boy's grab. He says to her as she heads back to the kitchen, "Rebecca." She turns around and he throws the cake hitting her square in the face. She starts to wipe the cake off her face and he demands, "pick it up." She lowers herself to the floor and picks up the remnants of the cake that fell there.

While in the kitchen she mops her face clean from the cake and looks in her pocket mirror. Despite this insult to her dignity, she reasons: "He is such a young boy to have lost his mother in a fire and his dad is now institutionalized from that loss. It is understandable that a child of tender years would act in this fashion. I probably would have acted the same way. He is just releasing his anger." Then she thinks more fervently on the subject and her mind wanders to the picture. "I need to get that picture out of his clutches. With that he can control me." She thinks, "tonight, while he is sleeping, I'll get it out of his end table where he keeps it in a jewelry box."

Her scheme is simple. Wait for the child to fall asleep, then go in and take it. But that jewelry box plays a song called "I will survive," and she can't have that playing when she seizes the picture. Stealthily, she goes into his room when he is downstairs and turns the volume off on the jewelry box. She thinks, "that'll outsmart him."

About 11:30 that night, she tip-toes into his room. Algar is sleeping soundly with his back to the target – the end table holding the jewelry box containing the picture. Craftily, she opens the end table and pulls out the jewelry box, opening it and the song, "I will survive" starts to play. She utters quietly "damn" and closes the box quickly. Algar slightly moves his left foot but remains in a dead sleep. She reopens it quickly and grabs the picture and shuts the box so only a few notes were played. She places it in the drawer and Algar starts to turn his head. Rebecca briskly makes her way to the door and closes it delicately.

She looks at the picture and taps her index finger against it saying, "you have brought me a lot of misery." She goes to her room and declares, "you will not control me anymore," as she rips it into many small fragmented pieces and flushes it down the toilet. Smiling she jumps on her bed and rests her head against the pillow looking upward at the ceiling, "I'm a force to be reckoned with."

That force was short-lived. The next morning Rebecca wakes up happy and marches downstairs to the kitchen, believing that Algar is still sleeping in his bedroom, only to find him at the dining room table holding a copy of the picture that was earlier destroyed. "You took my picture, didn't you?" Rebecca replies humbly, "no, no, I didn't." "You did. I heard you last night," he tells her. He adds, "for your sins, baptize yourself in shower water with clothes on, now. Then come back." Moments later, Rebecca returns soaking wet and dripping all over the floor. Hair is sopping wet. Algar says, "smile," as he takes pictures of her wet as she tries to muster a smile. "These pics will be on social media today," he declares.

Though the pictures were not revealing in any regard, they would tend to show that Rebecca has an unstable mind posting pictures of her wet yet fully clothed body with shoes on.

"You will not steal my pictures again," he commands. She answers, "yes."

Later that day, a girlfriend calls Rebecca. "Becky, why are you posting pictures of yourself in wet clothes?" She answers, "I didn't, the boy did. This is punishment for stealing his picture." The girlfriend asks, "what picture?" "I can't answer that," Rebecca proclaims.

That baptismal punishment became a regular basis for discipline for anything that Rebecca did thereafter. Every time she violated one of Algar's directives, she would undergo a baptism over clothes, which Algar would then post on social media. There were so many postings that the few girlfriends, Rebecca had, stopped contacting her thinking she had a fetish with wet clothes. Her only boyfriend moved on when he could never get a date with her because there was some obligation she had to fulfill at the residence, which Algar would impose minutes before the date.

She had become isolated and ostracized by her pictorials and general unavailability.

She now had to call him, "Sir," and she had to do his homework for his home schooling courses. This freed him up to do more important things, like video games and watching any shows he liked. She thought at times, "maybe I could poison his food or drink." But that would not keep her employed and probably end in her sentencing to death. Either option scared her enough to put that out of her mind.

One day, at lunch, Algar says, "I would like macaroni and cheese." Rebecca goes to the kitchen, returns and says, "it's all gone, sir." "Go to the store and get some, now." Rebecca answers, "yes, sir," and marches out the door. She was gone for about 1 hour. While away, she calls a priest saying, "I don't know what to do. This boy is controlling every step I take." The priest asks, "how old is the boy?" She answers, "7 years old." The priest states, "you can't control a 7-year old. Come on. Is he possessed?" She replies, "at times I think he is." "I'm not performing any exorcism for an answer as that. Go to counseling that is the best alternative," the priest finalizes. She replies, "he won't go."

When she returns home, she finds Algar sitting in front of the fireplace watching the flames rise. He is smiling as she enters the family room. "What are you burning, sir?" she asks. "Clothes, lots of clothes," is his answer. She screams, "those are my clothes, my clothes." Seeing them all in flames, she races upstairs to her room. She comes back with a Halloween costume that she wore for a party that is vintage pink poodle skirt and white short-sleeved blouse, both with poodles on them. "Is this what you want me to wear all the time around here?" she confronts Algar getting close to his face. "You could have asked me to wear it instead," she opines. Algar shows little reaction. "It's now the only thing that remains in my closet." Leaving in a huff, she turns toward the stairway and she hears Algar comment, "Rebecca, baptism." She turns around as if to rebuke him then, suddenly, she smiles and she says, "yes, sir."

Later, that evening, a posting goes out showing Rebecca drenched in a poodle skirt and blouse. Like the last posting, no one comments at all. She is completely estranged from the world. In one word, she is "contained."

CHAPTER SIXTEEN

Up For Investigation

Manny Tupelo is seated at a desk at the Miami-Dade Sheriff's Office near Pembroke Pines. Deputy Sheriff Jason Lazenby asks Manny, "could you describe this Peter guy." Manny relates, "well, it's kind of fuzzy. I just got off the boat from the rig and I was standing on the shore and this guy comes up to me and says he is interested in a rig like that," pointing to the rig in the bay. He then asks, "can you put me in touch with someone from your firm about purchasing such a rig?" And I answer him, "sure, his name is Monte. What's your name?" He says, "Peter." Jason asks, "how long did you talk?" "Not more than 3 minutes," Manny says. "Do you have any description of him at all?" implores Jason. "The only thing that comes to mind is that he was fair-skinned and about my height." "Any other distinguishing traits or blemishes?" asks Jason. Answering abruptly, Manny says, "no." "Can you do a composite sketch for me?" Manny answers, "I don't think so."

Without any leads, Jason goes to the location where the rig was operating when the alleged disappearance took place. At this time, there is only a missing person's report. The pad in the control unit of the rig has been wiped clean. Given this is bay water and fed by a river, it is quite likely that any blood traces would have been washed clean with time. That rig has been moved several times since the scene of his disappearance, which makes it difficult to place the rig at the exact spot it was when the disappearance occurred. Construction has moved along with the housing development, and Jason walks the fields for clues to Monte's disappearance. Based upon Manny's reports, he looks in the area that the rig was originally at and sees nothing in the water that points to foul play. Walking to the open field, he examines some debris-ladened soil and notes a small chip of a bone and a small torn fragment of clothing. Jason lifts his head and wonders why a clothing fragment is contained in this soil extracted from the bottom of the bay. He places it and the bone chip in a small plastic bag noting the time and place of recovery. He calls the County Forensic specialist and states, "I found something at the site but without a body or any other tangible evidence, we need verification. Could you take DNA samples from the Enright family so we can compare them with this bone chip? Thank you," says Jason.

CHAPTER SEVENTEEN

Board Reconsiders

Missing in action for over three months has caused the Board of Commissioners for the County to appoint a replacement to Monte Enright's council seat. Her name is Dorothea Gibbons and is delighted with the prospects of sitting as a Commissioner both literally and politically. She has always been an "unnamed" entity in the political field and rose to some notoriety when Enright was elected Commissioner, especially, in her role as his Assistant Campaign Manager. His then Campaign Manager was now working with a watchdog group in Washington, leaving Gibbons as the suitable replacement to appease the Enright constituency. Should Enright surface at some point she knows that she will have to step aside for his return. Nonetheless, she is thrilled with having the authority to vote on such important matters. But she has no shadow to speak of that she might cast to influence pact-voting. Without Enright visibly in the seat, the other land-locked districts are running "rogue." Their leader is gone and their loyalties now are easily influenced.

Douglas Jackson calls the meeting to order. "We have before us this evening is a reconsideration of the Arc of Tranquility as proposed by our Chief Engineer Seve Aguado. He has dropped the costs of the project down $100 million and has raised the escarpment wall 5 feet so that it sits above the current water level by 25 feet. That means it will cost the taxpayers and federal and state entities approximately $900 Million to build. Mr. Aguado is here to answer any questions concerning the project."

One Commissioner asks Aguado, "will it be visible from the shoreline?" Aguado answers, "yes, it will be. Just like any jetty it will be viewable from the shore." Another Commissioner asks, "will it be able to withstand Cat 5 hurricane force winds?" "Good question," says Aguado, "it can and will." Another Commissioner inquires, "will the water level inside the Arc remain a constant through the seasons?" Aguado states, "the Arc will have pumps throughout the system that remove excess water to a point outside of the Arc, so the water level does not exceed 25 feet below the top of the reef wall." "A follow-on question – will aquatic sports, sailing and boating be permitted?" Aguado answers, "yes, but surfing will be impacted as wave height and formation will be effected by the reef wall."

In her first day as Commissioner, Dorothea asked no questions. Other Commissioners had looked to her to see if she was going to advocate against the wall. When she sat silent, the others interpreted that she was not opposed to the wall.

When the vote was taken, 10 Districts voted for the project and 3 opposed, including Dorothea. With the passage of the project, Wade Terriff and Seve Aguado shake each other's hands vigorously, jubilant that they had won the project. The project would commence in 18 months' time once all the regulatory permits had been pulled and obtained.

If the Arc of Tranquility succeeded as planned, there was no stopping the political star of Seve from rising. He would be like Antoni Gaudi to the fabled Church of Sagrada Familia in Barcelona. He was on his way. But he needed to make sure nothing went wrong with this pet project; otherwise, he might find himself sinking like a stone below the waves of dissent, drowning in a fiasco of his own design.

CHAPTER EIGHTEEN

Tyesha's Terpsichore

Shortly after the interview, she was informed that she was hired as a Junior Economic Consultant just as Meghan had pronounced. She had other plans. She thinks, "I'm going to sail through the highest Senior Economic Consultant in the firm's shortest period of time." This ambition would require some stealth and tact. Thinking out loud in her bedroom the night before she embarks on her first day on the job at McElroy Management, "I must make a lasting impression." The weakest link is the easiest to break she thought. And her mind wanders to Prosperity Glendale. She plots that she would use the very essence of her dissertation at Harvard, "How subliminal messaging increases sales volume, unbeknownst to the customer." "I will incorporate the ASMR into the subliminal messaging format and create an economic program." She works diligently at the computer into the wee hours of the morning.

The next day arrives early and Tyesha is up early and raring to go. She stops by a florist's shop and buys some pink tulips on sale. Now she is armed to engage in office politics.

When she arrives to her Department, a staffer shows her to her desk. While seated at the desk, she begins the download of her computer software created the night before. She tests the program to see if it is up-and-running. It is and she smiles contently. She then starts exploring the work environs and happens upon hard-working Prosperity. She goes up to Prosperity's ear and gently says, "good morning." Somewhat startled Prosperity turns around and sees Tyesha. She smiles and says, "good morning to you. Your first day on the job." Tyesha jumps up and down, like a little girl, which pleases Prosperity. "I have a gift for you," Tyesha announces and then hands the pink tulips over to Prosperity. Whispering again in her ear, "you are worth all the gold in troy ounces everywhere in the world." Say it again with me, "you are worth all the gold in troy ounces everywhere in the world," as Prosperity joins with Tyesha. Tyesha then adds, "that is why you are named Prosperity." Prosperity joins the second-go-round, "and that is why I am named Prosperity."

Prosperity's guard is down and she listens to Tyesha closely. "I've just created a software that makes economics more interesting. You want to see it?" asks Tyesha.
Prosperity shakes her head and also says, "yes." Tyesha takes Prosperity by the hand and leads her over to her assigned computer. She sits Prosperity in her chair in front of the computer program.

"Press start," says Tyesha. The video shows a young girl who is disconnected from the world but loves numbers. She loves numbers so much, she can't leave them alone. Then, the program presents economic problems that have to be solved. This intrigues Prosperity to the point that she starts answering the formulations verbally and then enters the correct answers on the computer. Between each problem is a flash of subliminal information. It is not as persistent as a stroboscopic flash but one that appears during the answering process. For each correct answer, Tyesha's voice is heard on the program saying, "You are all gold, girl, believe in yourself." The flashing causes Prosperity to comment, "why does it flash?" Tyesha answers by stating, "it's either a software glitch or a sensor to ascertain if you are still playing along with the program." What Tyesha has not revealed is that the flash is filled with influencing data that can alter perceptions and attitudes. Encrypted in those flashes are packages of information encoding and endearing the viewer to the programmer and subtleties that encourage aberrant behavior. The aberrant behavior has not yet been defined by Tyesha. It is just suggestions that a person can experience greater individuality by breaking out of the norm and becoming one with herself. Tyesha watches Prosperity closely view the program getting closer to the screen. Tyesha did not anticipate that Prosperity would be so entranced with the program. Tyesha thinks "what will the results be for long-term viewing? Could it be harmful?" Her dissertation never covered the length of exposure to the messaging, just the results of such messaging. Tyesha bends over and whispers into Prosperity's ear, "what do you think of my program?" Prosperity has no reaction and refuses to take her gaze from the screen. Tyesha asks a second time, "what do you think of my program?" No reaction. Tyesha taps Prosperity's shoulder and she seems to come out of a spell, and she says, "It's good. I like it. Can I watch a little more?" "Sure," Tyesha bewildered, but given Prosperity's position as a Senior Economist, she is not one to argue, especially, on her first day on the job. Tyesha says, "you stay and watch and I'll get myself a cup of coffee." About a half hour later, Prosperity is still in front of the screen at Tyesha's desk. Tyesha thinks to herself, "the program is meant to repeat every two hours. I hope she will notice it's repeating and will go back to her station." When Tyesha stands up alongside of Prosperity, she asks, "can I watch a little longer?" Tyesha says, "of course." Then she adds, "you can watch as long as you like. Can I use your computer while you are at mine?" Prosperity says, "go ahead. My password is 'PG, I wish.'"

Tyesha checks back every few hours to see Prosperity enraptured with the program. Tyesha thinks, "gosh, she has been at it for hours. Doesn't she have assigned duties she must meet. She must have seen the program 3 times over and is not tiring of it." Finally, at the end of the day, Prosperity has a notebook full of the correct answers to the economic problems and gladly states, "that was 'fuckin' fun. Can you create a new one for tomorrow?" Tyesha displays a little puzzlement with the expletive uttered by Prosperity because she had read in the company manual that no profanity was to be used in the workplace. Nevertheless, she states, "did you like the software?" To which Prosperity answers, "love it. You're good." Tyesha then adds, "I will make a new software for tomorrow." "Thank you," says Prosperity.

Tyesha did not see Meghan that day but knew the encounter would come soon enough. What concerned her is, "what happens if I am discovered? What will that do if they find those flashes were conditioning human behavior?" She ruminates on that point and then resolves it by simply saying, "it is a program I developed at home and only brought it to work to show my ideas relative to sales volume. I can't help it that someone became infatuated with it." That response eases Tyesha's mind.

CHAPTER NINETEEN

More of the Same

Tired from the day's activities yet inspired by her subliminal messaging of Prosperity, Tyesha is rapturing over the prospects that she, in essence, is programming Prosperity. She thinks out loud, "I need to change this girl in a way that she will no longer be considered privately as the drab dresser." After a few moments of reflection, she hits on an idea and says, "this should win out." She will create a software package that has a "rewards-based system for correct answering." For every correct answer, the reward will be a "crypto-bauble" that converts into real money that is redeemable only for certain items of clothing – clothes that Tyesha determines to be sexy and/or fashionable. This "Cinderella" effect will transpose Prosperity from the "drab dresser" into a fashionista. Tyesha is so excited about this that she comments, "Prosperity will be my Barbie Doll to dress and accessorize." Embedded in the flashpoints now are cryptic cues to express her devotion and love for Tyesha.

The next day she arrives at work and is immediately greeted at her workstation by Prosperity, who asks, "did you bring a new program?" Tyesha answers, "yes, but can we allay some suspicion here. Can I download the program on your computer?" Prosperity replies, "you know my password –'PG, I wish.'" They both go over to Prosperity's computer and Tyesha downloads the program. As she walks away from that computer station, she whispers to Prosperity, "have fun." To which, Prosperity whispers back, "fuckin' fun," and laughs.

That whole day, Prosperity was glued to the program. Having been a long-term devoted employee and, now, high-level employee, she has proven herself over the years to be a conscientious worker that need not be monitored. Thus, there was no suspicion on anyone's part that she was playing and not working. Tyesha would happen by to see her obsessing over the program. She was fascinated with the software, seldom moving her eyes away from the screen. That night, Tyesha left a little late and noticed that Prosperity was still working the program after office lights turned off.

The next day, when Tyesha returns to work, there she is still playing the program wearing the clothes that she had worn the day before. Tyesha thinks, "this may be better if I let it run its course. Other than the flashpoints, it's a harmless program filled with incentives. Let's see if it has the projected outcome." At noontime, Tyesha walks to Prosperity's workstation and notes that she is gone. There is a lot of numbers scrolled on a yellow pad and a few coffee cups lying around the computer terminal. The computer is on and Tyesha notices that Prosperity had scored a high number of crypto-baubles. When converted, she exhales loudly, knowing that the converted real money did not exceed the balance in her bank account. But, other than those few tidbits of information, there is no other hint that the subliminal messages had worked their magic.

That was short-lived. Around 3 p.m. that day, Prosperity arrives in a stunning black, short cocktail dress causing other staffers to wonder if they had missed some formal event. At first shock had set in and staffers froze to make any comment at all. But eventually the improvement in her attire caused a gusher of accolades on how Prosperity looked. She is so happy. At one point, she starts dancing around jovially. The change in her behavior even causes eyebrows to raise questioning whether this was the same Prosperity, maybe, a happier twin, they had never met. When she sees Tyesha, she jumps into her arms and kisses her on the lips. Tyesha's eyes roll wondering if any co-workers saw that contact. "I am so happy. I love your game. I bought this and other wonderful clothes with my winnings. You have changed my life for the better," says Prosperity. "You've changed my life for the better." Tyesha happily responds, "I'm so glad you have awakened and see your true potential." Prosperity excitedly says, "I want to play this game a little longer. When I tire of it, can you make me a new game?" "Sure," says Tyesha.

While talking to Tyesha, some of the office girls pass by Prosperity and comment, "you look dazzling." Prosperity smiles back, "thank you." Looking at Tyesha and says, "My whole life has changed because of you. Can we go out some time and have a few drinks?" Tyesha wonders, "did I create the Frankenstein monster or what?" but then says, "Sure." "How about tonight?" Prosperity poses.   "It is a Friday night. I guess we can," offers Tyesha. "I'll meet you at McGallaher's Pub at 8," states Prosperity.

Later, in the evening as she prepares for the date, she wonders what will happen. "I know the program is good, but how good is it?" she thinks to herself. "Is this just two workers getting together to discuss office politics or is this something far worse – a romantic relationship? I don't want to get ensnared in a love triangle with Prosperity and Meghan – two people that hold the keys to my future ambitions with this firm. But, if I choose not to follow through with this meeting, will I set into motion a course of events that will eventually lead to my termination?" She resolves the conflict with the obvious answer, "I must go."

When they meet that night at McGallaher's, Prosperity is noticeably different. She now is wearing a very revealing outfit and pulls her chair really close to Tyesha. Tyesha thinks to herself, "this mad woman is suffocating me. What is she up to?" Prosperity closes in on Tyesha's cheek and kisses her softly at a point midway between the cheek and the ear. Tyesha smiles politely. Prosperity then says, "You are so attractive I can't believe my eyes. They are watering with so much enthusiasm." Those words seem to recheck Tyesha's mannerisms. She thinks, "I haven't ever had anyone say anything so nice to me. Male or female." She decides to wait it out for further comments from Prosperity. It doesn't take long before another salvo is fired. Prosperity sings, "Love abounds, where sands bleached by sun find two naked hearts that beat as one." Tyesha asks, "did you make that up?" "Yes, it was written in the stars," quips Prosperity as she kisses Tyesha on the lips. Tyesha is bewildered. "What do I do?" she thinks. "This is suddenly something definitely romantic. Is it sexual harassment? No," she answers quickly. She thinks, "this is someone who is interested in me. I don't feel it's harassment. We all want to be loved. Why do we always shoot the messenger? It's the rhapsody of love; a dance. Through some biological benediction, if a man, a woman, or even some other makeup, or a non-sexual, makes any suggestion or movement towards another person, we jump on it as if we are playing 'God,' trying to step into the path of God's creation and telling God 'to back off buddy.' Does that mean all creatures that engage in any ritualistic measures to seduce their counterparts for procreative purposes are engaged in sexual harassment? I won't play God and I won't countermand Prosperity for making a pass. It is God-given animal nature. It would be childish to complain. No one should be punished for making those overtures."

Tyesha and Prosperity talk for some time and listen to the music. After a couple of drinks, Tyesha starts having a good time and dances in place in her seat. She enjoys the attention that Prosperity is showering upon her. Prosperity's hand finally reaches Tyesha's thigh and Tyesha allows it to remain there. The evening ends with one final kiss. Tyesha is no longer confused but now realizes that she has power over the situation, more than she could ever imagine. If and when it becomes necessary, she has an assortment of ploys she can muster up on a moment's notice.

CHAPTER TWENTY

Enbryo's Punt

The criminal case of Dirk Rainjoy sheds some sunlight on the events that led Dirk to blow up SCI's warehouse. Certainly, desperation played its role in it. Faced with mounting expenses, investor frustration over R&D, and legal challenges to self-charging sensors, it was predictable that Dirk's emotional state was imploding in him to cause the destruction of the warehouse. What was truly puzzling is the almost careless and unplanned way it was orchestrated. It was like a zombie mouse who intentionally slows down to be captured by a hungry cat and devoured. When the Fort Worth Star-Telegram did a full expose on the Rainjoy case culminating in Dirk's pleading guilty to arson, destruction of private property, criminal mischief and violation of federal statutes, one reader took notice. Evelyn Wattig reads the digital version of the newspaper cover to cover every day. The story stoked her interest not so much as to the heinous nature of the destruction but on a couple of words found in the text "genetically shaped." She reads those words over and over trying to glean out a meaning that was innocuous. But the words were as clear as a just cleaned pane of glass. She attempted to contact the author of the article but was unable to reach him.

She has a personal stake in the matter. Her 16-year old son, Roland Wattig, has shown signs of criminal behavior. Not like blowing up buildings but more subtle ones. He is gifted in so many ways – academically, musically, and athletically. He became an accomplished guitarist at 11 years of age and was provisionally accepted on a waiting list to Juilliard School of Music. His chiseled features have prompted local photographers to send his pictures to top magazines in the country. He has not missed being on the Dean's Academic List for every quarter he has been in high school. Roland has developed a reputation for his talents that make him the envy of teachers, students and, even, their parents. His schedule is filled with so many activities, he cannot work and Evelyn wants him to achieve and not bother with work, which may distract him from her objectives for him. It may be the pressures of achieving that cause sudden outbursts of negative energy. The Wattig's Tom cat, "Tomalin," has been the family cat for a number of years. But there are times when Roland takes the sleeping cat by the paws and swings it round and round and releases it sending it into the wall. The cat's face has been bloodied by these acts of mayhem and has developed a slight limp when walking. Though she has not personally seen the acts, she has heard the cat's reaction and the thump against the wall. On a couple occasions, she has taken "Tomalin" to the vet to have stitches sutured on some of the deeper cuts. Roland tries to explain that the cat is afraid of him and, when he walks into the room, the cat runs into things to get away. Evelyn doesn't buy the story. What took her to the brink was on one occasion during an open-pit barbeque, Tomalin, as Roland reports, jumped into the pit suffering serious burns to his body. Having been a cat owner and lover for years, Evelyn knows that cats have a sixth sense when it comes to danger and will not clumsily submit to it. Other than having a perfect child, these recent developments have made her question whether genetic shaping had something to do with it. She determined when she was 41 years old that chances of finding a mate and have a natural child was probability-wise unlikely. She went to a fertility clinic and they got her in touch with Enbryo about genetically shaping. After undergoing gene shaping and IVF, 16 years ago Roland was born.

Having read the article on Rainjoy and not having any luck in speaking to the Star-Telegram, Evelyn calls Enbryo and speaks to its receptionist: "Is there someone there I can speak to about negative side effects of gene shaping?" The receptionist answers: "Yes. Dr. Marjorie Birmbaum. I'll connect you."

Eventually, Evelyn is speaking to Dr. Birmbaum and asks, "have there been any complaints from parents of genetically-shaped children regarding side effects?" not revealing her personal problems with Roland and Tomalin. Marjorie answers, "the only complaints are the typical ones that parents experience as their child grows up, such as not following rules, not doing homework, staying up too late, and not keeping their rooms clean and neat." Getting to the point, "has there been any complaint that a gene-shaped child is showing signs of physical abuse or destruction?" Marjorie goes to the topic of the day, "are you referring to the Rainjoy case out of Fort Worth?" Evelyn is surprised about the question and diffuses the focus and states, "not particularly. But has any parent had problems where the child shows a disregard for the law?" "No. There have been no studies conducted anywhere in the world that shows a correlation between genetically-shaped children and criminal propensity," Marjorie emphatically states. She further adds, "we really don't receive any complaints. Most of the time, the parents are calling saying, 'their child has been accepted' to Harvard, Stanford, MIT, or has just received his or her doctorate, or has made a startling invention." Defensively she continues, "during our formative years here at Enbyro we set up a complaint hotline and an ombudsman to handle grievances. As the years went by, no one complained about any child and, therefore, we terminated the hotline and fired the ombudsman. Overall, parents are happy with the results at Enbryo and we stand by our technology. Whatever happened in the Rainjoy case was caused by environmental circumstances unconnected to his genetic structure. I hope that answers your questions." Just about ready to hang up, Evelyn presses forward saying, "my son is hurting the family cat." Marjorie repeats, "your son is hurting the family cat?" "Yes," says Evelyn. "Then, you should contact the ASPCA or the authorities. That violates the law." Evelyn wonders, "do you think gene shaping caused that behavior?" Marjorie quickly answers, "no. Every time someone let's off some steam, doesn't translate to a genetic problem but one that is created by an environmental influence. I would recommend you take your son to a counselor and find out the source of his discontentment towards the cat." Evelyn says, "thank you" and then hangs up.

CHAPTER TWENTY-ONE

Dia's Private Parts

Business necessity required Dia to learn Spanish. Like so many things, she learned it quickly and was versant enough to get the job done. She speaks to Dr. Ignacio Mendez in a subdued tone using a cryptic kind of Spanish dialogue: "Necesito un 'neyed,' 'fem tra,' fem blad,' and 'splen." Dr. Mendez answers curtly, "tartare de encontrarlos [translate: "I will try to find them"]. Dia asserts, "los necesito tan rapido como puedas cosecharlos [translate: "I need them as fast as you can harvest them"]. She add, "alguien esta en su lecho de muerte" [translate: "Someone's on their death bed"].

Dr. Ignacio is an approximately 75-year old licensed medical doctor in Mexico with reciprocity to practice medicine in Texas, primarily in the El Paso area. He has staff privileges at El Paso General Hospital and a small office in that City. He regularly commutes between his medical offices in Ciudad Juarez and El Paso. The border custom agents know Dr. Mendez and allow him to pass without so much as showing his passport or driver's license. Many times, he tells the officers that he's taking his grandchildren for a ride into El Paso. Each time he does, they wave him through.

Later in the day, Dr. Ignacio meets with a Nicaraguan woman of 32 years in his offices at Ciudad Juarez. Her two children are seated in his reception area and the two boys, 8 and 9 years, are wrestling now and then on the floor of the reception. When their yelling gets out of line, their mother, Romina, raises her voice and says, "deja de gritar [translate: "Quit yelling"]. She then follows up and says, "no dejes que salga y te azote [translate: "Don't let me come out there and spank you"]. The boys snicker to themselves and then settle down sitting in the chairs provided.

Romina tells the doctor, "no tengo dinero para pagar el pasaje [translate: "I don't have money to pay for the passage"]. "Vine de Granada Nicaragua [translate: "I came from Granada, Nicaragua"]. She pleads with the Dr. holding his hand, "Quiero que mis hijos lleguen a Estados Unidos" [I want my boys to make it to America"]. The Doctor sums up, "como puedes llevar a tus hijos a Estados Unidos sin dinero? [translate: "How can you get your sons to America without money?"]. He states, "puedo ayudar si esta dispuesto a renunciar a un rinon o alguna otra parte del cuerpo" [translate: "I can help if you are willing to give up a kidney or some other body part"]. Concerned, she asks: "will that end my life" ["terminara eso con mi vida"]. He retorts, "por supuesto que no, su cuerpo funcionara normamente con un rinon, un ureter, una uretra y una vejiga" [translate: "Of course not, your body will function as normal with one kidney, one ureter, one urethra and one bladder"]. She consents, "De acuerdo, hagamoslo [translate: "okay, let's do it"]. The Doctor smiles and states, "lo programaremos para este proximo martes. El martes por la noche sus hijos estuaran en los Estados Unidos" [translate: "We will schedule it for this next Tuesday. Tuesday night your boys will be in the United States."

That next Tuesday, the surgery to remove Romina's left kidney and left ureter, along with the surreptitious removal of the spleen, takes place. It was uneventful performed at a local hospital in Ciudad Juarez. That night, while Romina is recovering from the surgery, Dr. Juarez drives across the border in the United States with Romina's two boys in his car. The border agent waves Dr. Mendez through.

CHAPTER TWENTY-TWO

Channeling the Canals of Death

The canals are dark and difficult to navigate. Not much light is offered up tonight. The balmy climate caused by a cloud-covered sky and warm trade winds make a perfect storm of dewpoint and rising humidity. The result is sweat breaks all over the face of Gizpaco as he tries to guide a modified gondola down these black waters. Trafalgar Bridge is farther down the waterway but so is the two pickups he must make. Usually, by the time he arrives to each pickup, the package is bagged and ready for delivery. He oars over to the side of the river and picks up the goods and goes to the next stop. He doesn't ask any questions because he knows the answers won't be forthcoming. The bags are placed by the side of the river and no one waits until he arrives. It's a silent task done without witnesses in the best possible light – total darkness. When the bags are placed in the bottom of the boat, they quietly take the ride without verbal reservation to the Trafalgar Bridge. The propeller of this boat is the sweeping motion of a single oar held by Gizpaco in a back-and-forth motion that moves the cargo and the boat through the still waters. He stops occasionally to mop his brow to keep the sweat out of his eyes. He tries not to think because it causes him to reflect upon his past and that does not bring him any joy. A blank mind gives little reason to revisit past events or to dream about an unlikely future. When he keeps his thoughts in the here and now, there is no pain or fear; he is living in the present. He looks for the occasional firefly to light up giving some dimension where he is in the journey to Trafalgar. There is a small bell on the side of the bridge that periodically rings – a gift from its maker signaling the bridge's looming approach for its river travelers. Gizpaco hears it in the distance and knows that he has one last pick up before it arrives.

As the last pickup approaches, the fireflies have deserted this portion of the river and Gizpaco is guided to the pickup spot solely by memory and the bend in the river. He directs the boat to the place where the pickup should be and lands the gondola. There is something mysterious about this pickup. Next to the bag sits a gentleman. Gizpaco sees the gentleman and shows no reaction. He grabs the bag and starts to cart it off. The gentleman attempts to grab Gizpaco's hand and his hand goes through the hand like air. The gentleman has only spiritual qualities. Gizpaco stares him in the face. The gentleman looks at the vacant, expressionless eyes of Gizpaco. That stare speaks volumes and the gentleman manages one word, "why?" Gizpaco, normally a man with no words, mutters inarticulately, "Life, death move in one direction." With tears in his eyes, the gentleman sits and cries, "I don't want to leave," transforming it into a question. "Come, I show you life," says Gizpaco. Gizpaco motions for the man to follow him, benevolently, and leads him and the sack to his gondola. They continue down the river to Trafalgar.

CHAPTER TWENTY-THREE

Playing Those Mind Games

Sabrina understands the concept. If she wants at his money, she's got to put some distance between Glen and Jan. She worries a little that the DTM may have worn off since the last visit. She decides to confirm the massage for the following Monday. Dialing the number, Sabrina feels like a black panther ready to pounce on her unsuspecting kill. "Hi, Jan, this is Sabrina," she announces. "Hello, Sabrina, how are you?" Jan replies. "I'm confirming your appointment for next Monday. Are you planning on being here?" Sabrina inquires. "Of course," says Jan, "and I'll be wearing that green and white dress with white nylons. It took some time to locate but I finally found the nylons. Not easy." Sabrina laughs and says, "that's great. I didn't think you were really listening." "If that gets me the best massage imaginable, I would wear the sun on my back," she quips. Both ladies laugh. Then, Sabrina turns to a more subtle, sinister direction and asks, "you know what would be good for you is to wear your hair platinum with streaks of blonde tinged in and blue eye shadow." Jan remarks, "Glen doesn't like eye shadow and make up other than lipstick. He likes my hair color now, brown. He's always been attracted to brunettes." Sabrina filled with a vitality adds, "we all need change. Surprise him with the additional make-up and hair color." Before Jan could add anything further to the request, Sabrina concludes, "I'll see you both on Monday. Bye."

Monday arrives and Sabrina is poised and ready to spring into action. Jan and Glen come into Mid-Apple Massage quarreling over something a little obtuse but does not involve herself into it. She will explore it more when they are a little more sedated. "Good morning, Jan and Glen. Are you ready for a muscle-moving extravaganza?" Sabrina asks cheerfully. Before an answer elicits, Jan says, "how do I look?" She is wearing a green and white dress with white nylons, blue eye shadow and, as requested, platinum hair with blonde streaks. "You look incredible. It lights up your face and the outfit is stunning," comments Sabrina. This causes Jan to blush for the first time in a long time. She has derived some attention over her appearance. She is delighted. They both embrace and jump together like teenagers over the sight. Jan is radiantly happy. This is a far cry from the disposition of Glen. He sulks over the change. "I told her I don't like eye shadow or that hair color but she didn't listen to me." Sabrina allows Glen to vent a little more. She knows from his profile that he was the one that garners a lot of the attention through maintaining his youthfulness and now that Jan is dressing it up may take some of the limelight away from him. He is irritated for a moment. "We have been married for 45 years and now she doesn't want to listen to me." That is the clue Sabrina needs to assure him he is still the star. She goes over to him and hugs him tightly and places her hand on his butt and says, "the massage today will heal those ill feelings. Just you wait." Jan sees the contact and thinks to herself, "Sabrina is such a nice lady to make my husband accept some change in my life." Sabrina then announces, "each of you off to your respective dressing rooms and meet me here with towels only."

The two return to the massage tables in better temperament than before. They both lie face down on the massage tables waiting for the oils and balm. Glen extends his arm out to Jan to grab hold of it and, before she can reciprocate, Sabrina pulls Jan's arm back in and takes Glen's hand and places it by his side saying, "this is a massage. No hand holding. It makes it difficult to do my job."

Given Glen's negative deportment, Sabrina elects to massage Glen first to reduce the anxiety from his recent rankling. Sabrina wonders, "did the effects of the last DTM wear off on him so that I need to apply more denatured balm and suggestion? How can I be sure? Is there a way to test?" She thinks of a way to introduce the subject and asks, "is there something different that you would like me to do this time?" That question takes him by surprise but he answers, "no. Last time was very good." Sabrina asks, "what did you think about during that massage?" "I thought of freedom and, and you," stumbling to get the words out. Sabrina assures him, "that is what a massage is all about getting those feelings out," as she places his hand on her breast and says, "it's got to come from the heart." He starts to pull away and then she puts his hand back on the spot, "it's the heart that counts."

Not seeing the contact, Jan heard the entire conversation and lifts her head up and says, "it's the heart that counts." Assuming that Jan had not only heard but saw the contact and didn't complain meant to Glen that she was alright with him touching Sabrina in an intimate way during the massage. That would change the shape of things to come.

Sabrina initially applies the denatured balm and other oils to the back and neck of both Glen and Jan to induce some twilight level of unconsciousness. When both have reached that stage of somnolence, she begins the massage process on Glen's backside removing the towel completely from his body. Again, she has him turn over, drowsy and semi-conscious. Sabrina notes, "he has a chiseled body for his early 80's and his package seems worthy." Her trance suggestions are stronger than the last time and she whispers: "You desire me more than your wife. When you see that platinum hair and eye shadow worn by your wife, you will think only of me. Your passion to kiss me is overpowering and you want desperately to touch me right in front of your wife. As a matter of fact, you get pleasure having your wife see you making advances at me. You don't care what she thinks." Sabrina repeats these lines over and over in whispered tones into Glen's ears. She then finishes by saying, "you want to kiss me right now, don't you?" She puts her lips down on his lips but makes no movement to kiss. Glen starts kissing Sabrina uncontrollably, which goes on for 5 minutes. Sabrina carefully takes pictures of the kissing and seals them away for future reference in the iCloud. When the kissing stops, Sabrina adds, whisperingly, "your wife really enjoys seeing you kiss me and that you should do it regularly when she is around. It heightens your level of arousal. Now just relax for the moment." As Glen rests, Sabrina moves to Jan.

She massages the backside of Jan and whispers so gently into her ear, "you look absolutely beautiful tonight. You want the world to see that you are so beautiful and you want to dress up all the time in girly things." Sabrina removes the towel covering Jan and strokes her legs and buttocks. "You know that women are different from men and you want to be different. Sometimes a husband can get in the way of you being beautiful. Always please yourself first and remember your husband is always second in your life. Go ahead and try to say it with me, "your husband is always second." Jan mumbles but apparently hears the suggestion. "Let's turn you over, Jan," as she helps Jan turn over. She continues whispering in her ear, "You love my advice and you don't like to hear your husband's advice. It's usually wrong because he doesn't consider your feelings first. You recognize that I consider your feelings first. As your shaman, you notice that I have lots of friends and everyone likes me. Say it, 'everyone likes me.'" Jan mumbles again. Sabrina continues with the DTM suggestions and says: "After your massage today, you notice that your husband likes me physically but that isn't important to you. What's important to you is that you and I have a spiritual love that transcends physical love. Men tend to express things in physical terms; whereas, women, like you and me, have a much deeper sense of love. Physical love like men want only last temporarily; whereas, our spiritual love will last and last." She repeats this as she slowly rubs Jan's body. Then, as the final measure of suggestion, she touches Jan's nipples and says as she bounces her fingertip from one nipple to the next, "we have new terms for endearment now. Because of our special closeness, we will call each other "honey" because we are so sweet to each other and we savor our spiritual love so dearly. Help me say it together, 'honey.'" Say it Jan, "honey," and this time Jan says, "honey" quite audibly. She goes on to bounce from one nipple to the next as she makes her next point, "your husband is really physically interested in me. The more he shows interest, it makes it difficult for you to remember his name. It is far easier for you to call him "money," because he has so much of it. When he shows interest in me, you will call him 'money.' Let's say it together, 'money.' Jan mouths it and then says it loudly, "money," as Sabrina looks over to Glen. She continues to repeat it over and over, "money for "honey," "money for honey."

45 minutes pass and the two come out of the DTM and the reactions are about the same as the first time, except the focal point is no longer the husband and wife but Sabrina. Jan looks at Sabrina in awe like she is the high priestess and marvels at everything that comes out of her mouth. Given that Jan is the first fully aware and awake, Sabrina comes over a gives a hearty hug, which lasts for several minutes. She tells Jan to wear some high heels and a brilliant crimson dress with nude nylons. Jan answers, "I will and would love to please you." "Remember," Sabrina says, "what we talked about. You first; money second." Jan stops and thinks for a moment like she is having difficulty remembering and then it hits her, "I remember now."

When Glen fully awakens, he seems exhilarated in other ways. He stands up naked and declines the towel being offered by Sabrina. Sabrina and Jan laugh at the refusal. As he was coming out of the stupor, he did see Sabrina and Jan in a long embrace and, so, he saunters over to Sabrina and extends his arms out and Sabrina gives him a hug. She takes his hand and places it on her rump and that's all it takes for Glen to start kissing Sabrina. Sabrina does not kiss back giving the impression that this is all Glen's doing. She glances at Jan and both eye each other with a certain sense that they operate at a higher level of human consciousness; that this is the base form that men operate from. After the sustained kissing, Sabrina breaks away and says, "let's hold hands together" with Jan holding Sabrina's right hand and Glen holding Sabrina's left hand. Sabrina exploits the opportunity that she has indulged by pushing the needle point closer to the fractious edge by saying, "until our next massage, let us remember that "money is for honey; honey is for money." They all recite the mantra with a quizzical look on Glen's face on what it all means, but he still goes along with it, especially, after kissing Sabrina so intimately for so long in the presence of his wife.

Though they came together to the massage, once Sabrina lets go of the couple's hands, they both retreat to their own dressing rooms as if they never had known each other.

CHAPTER TWENTY-FOUR

Shaved and Confused

It is a good morning for Rebecca. She has gazed at her bank account and realizes she is closer to leaving this humiliating employment. Soon, she will be in her own place with a new station in life and, possibly, new employment that will have no hint or trace of childcare. She has endured enough. Contemplating the end game, and while she is in her room, she utters out loud, "I'll sue him for everything he has done to me. He's a loaded little child. I'll help myself to some of his millions." Thinking about his millions, she goes to his checking account online with a local bank. She knows his password because the money is only used for necessities of life and emergencies. It's more for day-to-day needs and does not contain anywhere close to the bulk of his liquid assets, including his cash accounts. She looks at the balance of this account which contains $22,536 and wishes she could take that money and run off into the darkness never to set foot in this mansion again. Then, with the movement of the cursor she transfers money from his account to her account. Not a large sum, but $250 won't be determined as excessive for any reason. She has done this on numerous occasions as she gets more and more anxious to leave. She will claim it was for food and general supplies. That has worked in the past with the child's private accountant and she reasonably believes this time will be no exception.

Algar is in the kitchen making a strong brew of chamomile tea.

He has been thinking that his meter reading as of late with Rebecca is she's too happy, and that she is plotting something sinister. He must counterpunch and quick. He thinks, "dad used to use some pill that would make him sleep better after mom was burnt to the death. I think I saw the container in his medicine cabinet recently." He scampers upstairs and retrieves the bottle. He opens it and takes three. He is not a good reader but notes in large letters, "helps sleep." The bottle contains the name of the contents, Secobarbital Sodium Capsules. He plops the three capsules into a pink tea mug, "Viva La Difference." The other tea mug is in red, which reads on the outside, "This Lady's in Red." He takes the two mugs to the nearby dining room table and sits down with his hands folded together.

Humming as she comes downstairs, feeling a "new and fresh air" of change in the midst, she walks into the kitchen happy and then spies his presence. Softening the sounds of her hum, she says, "what would you like for breakfast?" Algar answers, "just tea. I made some for us. Pick one and we'll toast a new day." Her face drops 8 floors from happy to troubled. This resurrected soul is being pushed back into the grave of uncertainty. She looks down into the mugs wondering what if anything is in there other than tea, but she quickly responds, "I probably shouldn't have. Do you know how to make tea?" Studying the contents closely. He answers, "my mom used to boil water and put the tea bag in. It's simple." This may be the toughest choice of her life. She thinks, "why is he doing this? He has never done anything for me that was nice. I have a 50-50 chance as to my choice. It's like black or white." She looks at the position of each mug trying to ascertain if one is closer to Algar, which might reveal his preference for the mug. But, she thinks, "maybe I should let him choose, then go for the one he selects." She further thinks, "I'm a grown adult I should be able to outsmart this child. I'll have him select." She announces to Algar, "since you were nice enough to make the tea, why don't you select the mug of your choice." Algar reaches for the Pink mug but before he can get his hand on the mug handle, Rebecca says, while grabbing the Pink mug, "Pink is my favorite color. It's what makes us different," pointing to the printing on the outside of the mug.

Algar grabs the Red mug and clangs out a toast with Rebecca with her saying, "to a brand new day." Reticently, Rebecca drinks the tea slowly, tasting whether it may contain contents other than tea byproducts. The smell of the chamomile is strong and sweet and dominates the sense of smell over taste. Both consume the contents in short order. Both are seated in high back leather chairs at a circular glass dining table; one of three in the household and one more conducive to quick meals at or near the kitchen. By the time she finishes the last drop of the tea, her eyes are at half-mast and she lays back into the chair wondering why she is so lethargic. She mutters, "I must not have had enough sleep last night. I'm really tired. I'll just rest here." She places her hands in her lap and falls into a deep sleep. The boy goes over and raises her hand and arm and then let's go causing her arm and hand to drop to her lap again. He then gets a hair clipper that his father used to cut his hair and he buzzes off her hair while she sleeps and throws her hair in the fireplace creating a pungent smell that fills the living room.

After this he waits for Rebecca to wake up. In the meantime, he receives a call from Jerry Minkow, his private accountant. "She did it again," he exclaims. "What," asks Algar. "She sent money from your account to her account this morning," adds Jerry. He goes on to say, "she has done this at least 18 times in the last 6 months." Algar asks, "what should I do?" Jerry answers, "call the authorities." Algar says, "go ahead."

She slowly comes out of her sleep – a sleep she has been in for about 5 hours. When she wakes up she rubs her face and looks around. She does not see Algar. The two tea mugs are gone and have been thoroughly washed. She moves her hand to stroke her hair. She thinks, "it's gone," and then shouts out, "it's gone." She runs through the house trying to find Algar and to confront him about the hair shave. She finds him in the library looking at paintings in a book on the Napoleonic Wars. "You cut my hair you crazed and inconsiderate child. You drugged me and then shaved my head. I'm going to sue you for this." She looks in the mirror and she cries at seeing her long hair gone and her face looking far less than appealing to the eyes. "I'm going to get you for this." She picks up her phone and tries to call the police at the local station. The Desk Sergeant says, "ma'am, we know about the situation and we have an armed patrol unit heading to your place. Be patient." Rebecca says, "now is your day to pay the piper. They're coming to get you," laughing out loud. "My days of punishment and rebuke are over," she adds.

In a very mild-mannered tone, Algar says, "Rebecca, baptism." She responds, "no more baptisms; I haven't sinned. You have." He repeats, "Rebecca, baptism." "No," she quips, "I will not."

A knock comes on the door and Rebecca races to open it. "Finally, officers, you have arrived. The boy is right there. Arrest him." Both officers look at Rebecca with a recently shaved scalp. "Ma'am, do you have any disability or condition that requires special accommodation?" "No," she quips, "I'm perfectly healthy and normal. He isn't." She sees that they are looking at her scalp. "He did this to me. He cut my hair off," she argues. They look over at the 7-year old and he puts on his most innocent face a child could display. Police Officer Al Williams says, "the boy cut your hair?" "Yes, and he drugged me," she clamors out. "This boy did this to you?" asks the other officer Sam Cunningham. "Yes," she pleads with them. "Ma'am, we are not here for a domestic dispute between you and a child of tender years. We are here to arrest YOU for defalcation of funds and embezzlement," Sam states. "What," she states, "I've done nothing wrong. I'm innocent." "We have a sworn affidavit from the private accountant testifying under oath that you have taken money from this poor boy's bank account. That's embezzlement," says Al Williams. Sam says, "you can tell your story to the judge."

Sam attempts to place the zip cuffs on Rebecca but she runs away and manages to get outside. The officers are running after her and she slips on some cobblestones near the pool and falls in. She comes out of the pool completely soaking wet as Officer Al places the handcuffs on Rebecca. "By the way, you are now facing an additional charge for resisting arrest," says Al. Just as they lead Rebecca out of the house, Algar takes a picture of Rebecca soaking wet with head shaved and police escorting her out the door handcuffs and all. That picture was posted on a social media platform that day. No one commented. No one is following her anymore.

CHAPTER TWENTY-FIVE

It's A Match

Deputy Sheriff Jason Lazenby's tells his investigator, "get out to that construction site before all evidence is placed in concrete. Their third phase is going in soon and we have limited time to investigate." The Investigator named Reed says, "the case went cold and now the developer is pressing his contacts in the Mayor's office to approve the third phase." "Reed," says Jason, "we all know this. See if you can find any hard evidence that will survive legal challenge." He adds, "with the DNA report showing a match, we now know the deceased is Monte Enright. It seems most apparent, given the fine bone fragments, that the rig was the death instrument.

Find out who knew how to operate the rig. Also, find out who his friends and enemies were."

After going to the construction site and hiring a deep sea diver, they could find very little evidence of what happened. The workers knew nothing about the dredging of the bay but admitted that the site was now buried under a concrete foundation. They contacted Manny at Enright Way and asked to see the rig up close and personal. Reed goes out and examines the rig from a dry dock looking at the teeth of the cutter. He comments to Manny, "do you know anyone surviving contact with the cutter?" Manny looks at Reed and laughs, "look at those swirling teeth. Could you survive an encounter with them?" Reed answers, "no."

Through District 5, Reed learned that Monte was opposed to the Arc of Tranquility, project back by the County's Chief Engineer, Seve, and, while on the Commission, Monte voted the project down, which influenced other member Districts to do the same. Without Monte, the project passed with flying colors.

It was a long shot but Reed contacts Seve in person and inquires, "I'm investigating the death of Monte Enright and wanted to know if you had any involvement with him in the days that preceded his death." "Not really," says Seve, "the last time I saw him was at a Commission meeting." Reed asks, "did you exchange any harsh words with him when the Arc of Tranquility was voted down?" Seve was taken aback by the question because authorities now may be connecting the two together. "Of course," says Seve, "we got along extremely well." Reed agrees, "I heard the two of you did get along, joking a lot." Seve says, "yes. We were friends." Then, Reed hits with the most poignant question, "do you have any Russian friends?" Seve was blown away with that question and hesitates in answering, "there is a lot of Russians that live and work in South Florida and I have met my fair share of them, but I would not say I have any friends who are Russian." "Just as I thought," says Reed.

Feeling that he had answered brilliantly that last question, Seve believes he has escape further scrutiny, but the next question really hurt: "Was it easier for the Arc project to be approved because Monte was no longer on the Commission?" Seve responds, "I don't know one way or another. I lowered the budget by $100 million and that was enough to convince other District Commissioners to vote for the project." Reed agrees, "I heard the project is a decent project that we need in all of South Florida. As the water rises, tempers begin to flare," he pontificates and then adds, "on both sides of the argument. Were you mad at Monte for voting against you?" "No," answers Seve, "as I said before." Reed finishes and says, "Thank you for your help."

CHAPTER TWENTY-SIX

Prosperity Blooms

Tyesha feels she's working a double shift and thinks: "How much longer am I going to continue serving up my economic workload at the office during the day and then programming my superior after hours at night? It's a lot of work and exhausting my bank accounts with the rewards that are given to Prosperity for right answers." She mulls the question over and then answers to herself, "Prosperity is so easily malleable she will be my queen pawn to move around this chess board. But her infatuation with me is a little disturbing. But, I do it with men, why can't I do it with women."

Her thoughts change to Meghan Middlebrook. She hasn't seen her since the interview and the welcoming to the staff. "I know she works in another department but she has not come around. Maybe that's better. If she did, could she be programmed as Prosperity? No, no, she's way too smart to fall into such a trap. How do I get charge over her?" Tyesha decides to step up the programming of Prosperity and use her as a tool for change.

This night she programs in subtle clues that beauty mandates flagrant displays of promiscuity to make the room light up with one's presence. Subliminal suggestions advocate displaying sexuality in creative ways. Smoking a joint and general playfulness advance beauty in unique ways. Then, she suggests that such displays are Pavlovian in creating a wholesome work environment and keeping the job upbeat. She always finishes each program with conditioning to show affection and, above all else, loyalty to Tyesha, the programmer.

Prosperity has changed 180 degrees since Tyesha happened upon her life. The Rules at McElroy Management are largely ignored these days by Prosperity. The usual course of business is for Tyesha to get to work at 8 a.m. and download the program onto Prosperity's computer. Prosperity comes in at 9:30 a.m. or as late as 10:30 a.m., goes to her computer and plays the new program for the rest of the day. Tyesha then works on her assignments handed down by the Senior Economist in the Development Department. On this particular day, Prosperity is wearing a white dress with a zipper down the front from just below the neckline to the navel. She rushes over to Tyesha at her desk and Tyesha stands up to greet her. Prosperity hugs onto Tyesha like clinging to the side of a life raft and asks, "what do you think about the dress?" Tyesha responds, "it's beautiful and especially with you in it." Hearing that, Prosperity re-engages the hug then pulls back and seductively states: "I can control the level of its sexualosity, pulling down the zipper from the neckline to just above her navel." "Wow, that will get a lot of eyes looking," Tyesha noticing that a portion of her breasts has popped out. "It should and will. I'm off to my computer happily," says Prosperity, skipping but not zipping her dress back up. Tyesha rolls her eyes but then hastens a smile at the sight of the girl skipping to her workstation.

About 4 hours later and after lunchtime, Prosperity returns to Tyesha's computer and says, "I love this program. This is the best so far," rubbing Tyesha's back as she speaks. Tyesha responds, "oh, that feels so good." Prosperity adds, "you want me to do the front?" "Oh, no," Tyesha counters, "that might be a tad out of place here." "Well, if you ever want it, you know where I sit," Prosperity laughingly states. She then adds whispering into Tyesha's ear, "I'm gonna buy a joint. If anyone asks, tell them, 'I just stepped out for a moment.'" Tyesha says, "you got it girl." Tyesha says, "maybe you should" gesturing the zipper on her white dress upward with her hand. "Fuck no, when someone is beautiful, she needs to show it." With that Prosperity races off.

While Prosperity was out and about, an unidentified co-worker dropped off a message written on a scrap of paper, saying "I love your rack."

Later that day, Prosperity is seated at her desk with her legs spread around the computer she works at smoking a joint. The scrap of paper has been taped to the side of the computer as she glances at it periodically and smiles. Her mind moves the cursor around the computer screen and she exclaims, "another right answer. Moolah, Moolah." The joint wafts into the ventilation system causing one of the office managers to smell the marijuana scent and to go investigate. By the time she gets to Prosperity's wing of the building, the MJ has been butted out and Prosperity's legs had returned to underneath her desk. What the office manager sees is the typically diligent working Senior Economist Prosperity advancing the business requirements of McElroy. Unable to find the locus of the joint, she concludes it must have originated from another company's offices.

CHAPTER TWENTY-SEVEN

Review and Reward

Meghan glances at the 6-month performance evaluation of Tyesha Biggerstaff and notes that it makes a recommendation for promotion to Senior Economist. She examines the report in detail and notes that on every subject criteria from personal interactions with workers and clients to quality and quantity of work performed have designations of "exceptional" -- the highest marks that can be given by a supervisor. Meghan looks at the signature of the supervisor and it is Prosperity Glendale. Meghan is disturbed by the recommendation for promotion because no one in the history of the company went from Junior Economic Consultant to Senior Economist in the span of a 6-month period.

She decides to meet with Prosperity and find out the underpinnings for the recommendation. She walks over to Prosperity's wing and finds Prosperity hard at work on some project wearing a cute black cocktail dress with black nylons. "When did your sense in fashion change?" asks Meghan mindful that Prosperity is a senior employee at the firm with 6 years more seniority than she. "Just recently," answers Prosperity. Not wanting to send up a flare of discontent, Meghan supportingly states, "you look stunning in it." "Thank you," says Prosperity, taking her eyes off the monitor and looking at Meghan.

With that as a cue, Meghan asks holding Tyesha's performance evaluation, "why do you recommend her for a Senior Economist position?" Prosperity replies, "she is a hard-working girl with an excellent aptitude for economic theory and great academic credentials." Meghan offers, "I don't deny that her credentials are anything less than stupendous but that isn't the point. If we promote people during their probationary period to top economists aren't we telling those who put in the time that experience and devotion are meaningless?" Prosperity retorts, "Tyesha deserves this promotion early. We want to keep her here and not have some fuckin' money grubbing competitor seize her up. She is a gold doubloon on a shiny blue sea floor." Meghan dismisses the profanity remark as a hyperbolic statement to support her position. "I only ask that you reconsider your evaluation as to recommending to a higher position. You can give her the "exceptional" ratings but not the promotion," she suggests to Prosperity.

Prosperity gets tough and argues, "I will make my recommendation to promote anyone I believe is qualified for the position." Meghan argues, "she may be qualified but not after 6 months of work here. It is ridiculous for you to make such a recommendation. Even if she was bringing in one or more major clients, still that would not be reason enough to promote her to a Senior Economist position."

"Look it, you could do whatever you want with the employees you supervise. I won't interfere with that evaluation or any recommendations. This is my employee and I choose to evaluate her based upon my personal observations of her work performance and, if I see fit, she is deserving of a raise or promotion, I will make the necessary recommendations. Stay out of my business," exclaims Prosperity.

Angry at Prosperity's tough stance, Meghan states, "Well, I'm not going to be standing still on this, Prosperity. If you do not retract the recommendation, I am going to call a Senior Economist meeting and override your recommendation because it fails to take seniority into consideration," Meghan pontificates.

"You do whatever you think is fair in your mind, but I am still going forward with the recommendation," quips Prosperity.

Irritated to the point of being angry, Meghan states, "don't use profanity in the workplace. Need I tell you that."

Prosperity counters, "I'll fuckin' say whatever I want and those rules you can shove up your ass."

Alarmed by the reply, Meghan walks away.

Later that day, Prosperity informs Tyesha that Meghan is going to block her promotion to Senior Economist. Tyesha replies, "we'll see about that."

CHAPTER TWENTY-EIGHT

Jailhouse Blues

Rebecca has been assigned a public defender, Bruce Rochester, an experienced trial attorney that has a reputation of being a solid fighter for his criminal clients. He doesn't do it for the money; the money never pays enough. He does it for the "thrill." The thrill to slip the entire carpeting from underneath the prosecution's case causing it to collapse. It has happened many times over the years and Deputy District Attorneys respect his viewpoint immeasurably. They know that if they don't heed his words by the seventh day of trial something biblical will take place – he calls it playing with the "seventh." Bruce ties it into his philosophy, "on the Seventh Day God rested; on the Seventh Day Bruce rested inferring that once he rested his case, the prosecution's case will be left in shambles. This has haunted a lot of prosecutors to find a solution to the charges and forego taking the ultimate descent into trial.

This morning sees Rebecca in the visitor's section of the jail house. "Hi," Bruce introduces, "I'm Bruce Rochester and I have been assigned to be your attorney." Rebecca with head shaved and some scratches on her arm wearing orange jail suit says, "good morning, sir." Somewhat empathetic, "I see you have some scratches on your arm. Do you want those treated?" he asks. "No, I will survive." Then he chuckles a bit, "I heard you took a swim before your arrest." She doesn't even smile at the remark but fretfully claims, "I was set up. I had to run." Realizing

Rebecca is taking this far too seriously, Bruce adjusts course and says, "I've read the report and the private accountant's affidavit. To be convicted on this doesn't require substantial evidence. They parade the accountant on the stand, they show the withdrawals from Algar's account to your account, and, *voila,* you're guilty as charged. Because of the amount of money involved, I cannot get this placed into diversion or have it reduced to a misdemeanor. I know you are a first time offender but the child was under your care and you took advantage of the situation to steal from him. My office has hired an investigator to look at financial records and electronic transfers of funds to find out if there are any potential glitches that could make this a defensible case."

Changing subjects, "It may be several months before this case goes to trial and you will be cooling your heels in this jailhouse. Do you have someone that can post bail on $100,000 bond?" he asks. "No. I have no friends. I have lost them all because of that deceitful child," getting angrier by the moment and adding, "he can't do this to me and get away with it." Bruce retorts, "for Christ's sake, he's a 7-year old boy."

"I will schedule a bond hearing with the Court and see if we can drive the bond down or out of existence. I will put you on the stand to testify that you are not a "flight risk." "Okay?" he looks at Rebecca. Rebecca answers, "okay."

CHAPTER TWENTY-NINE

Under Protective Custody

The Clerk announces, "People v. Rebecca DeBlaine." Judge Preston states, with the District Attorney on one side and Bruce on the other side of counsel's table, "Counsel," looking at Bruce, "you have a motion on calendar to reduce bail or release the Defendant on her own recognizance. You tell me that you are going to put the Defendant on instead of through declaration, is that right?" "Yes, Your Honor," says Bruce. "Have you advised her of her right against self-incrimination?" asks the Judge. "I have," Bruce responds, "and I am limiting the area of testimony to "flight risk." Judge replies, "Proceed."

Bruce: Now, Ms. DeBlaine, do you have any resources to pay bail in this matter?

Rebecca: No, I do not. I'm broke.

Bruce: Do you have any friends or relatives that could post bail for you?

Rebecca: No, I do not. My friends are all gone.

Bruce: Where were you born?

Rebecca: Clementsville, Kentucky.

Bruce: Do you have any family remaining there?

Rebecca: I do not.

Bruce: Have you ever lived or traveled outside the United States?

Rebecca: No, I haven't.

Bruce: Do you have any former friends or relatives that live outside the USA?

Rebecca: No, I do not.

Bruce: Do you have plans to leave this country because of the pending charges?

Rebecca: No, I do not.

Bruce: Do you have the financial ability to leave this country?

Rebecca: No, I don't; I'm broke.

Bruce: Would it help for your defense if you could be released from custody?

Rebecca: Yes.

Bruce argues, "your Honor, Ms. DeBlaine is not a 'flight risk.' She knows no one, either friend or relative, that can assist her in making bail or provide a haven to avoid the prosecution of this case." Judge Preston interrupts Bruce's argument, "we would still try this case in her absence anyway," looking at Rebecca. Bruce nods his head in agreement. Bruce continues, "she could end up serving her entire sentence for these charges before her case comes to trial. That is plainly wrong." Judge smiles a little and then says, "then we'll miss the 'Seventh." Realizing the Judge isn't buying his argument, he states, "we'll submit."

Judge pronounces, "Your argument, Counsel, is compelling but so is the offense. While she was the child's caretaker, it is alleged she stole from his account on a regular basis. This is a serious violation of trust. Those funds were to be used to provide for the child." Rebecca starts to speak up, "but ..." before she could get the words out Bruce says, "be quiet." The Judge continues, "I don't necessarily see a flight risk but I'm not sure she is willing to stand trial given the fact that she resisted arrest and started running from the officers before falling into the pool. I'm going to deny your motion."

Just as Bruce is about to walk away, the Judge adds: "but, I have received a letter from the victim, Algar Puccini, written with the assistance of his corporate counsel and it is a very compelling piece of evidence," causing Bruce's eyebrows to rise. Judge continues, "he makes a generous invitation given the financial problems that beset Ms. DeBlaine." He states," as the Judge reads from the letter, "I know the precarious position Rebecca DeBlaine is in. I don't excuse her from stealing from me and would hope that the continued prosecution of the case would make her realize the gravity of the offense, but, in my own way, I appeal to the good conscience of the Court to release her to my protective custody rather than her continued incarceration until trial occurs."

The Judge puts down the paper on the bench and states: I have known Theodore Puccini for a number of years attending Judges' nights and other functions, and he was such a generous man with his time and his money. It is so tragic that his wife was killed in that unfortunate accident and now with his father being institutionalized the boy has no one to love and care for him. The very person he placed his trust in has allegedly stolen from him. The boy has access to an army of corporate officers, attorneys and accountants to guide him through this narrow strait. I am going to make the following orders:

1. Rebecca is released to the protective custody of Algar Puccini;

2. This confinement will be treated as part of any sentence should she later be found guilty of the alleged offenses and credit will be given for that time;

3. She is to obey all house rules and any directions that Mr. Puccini and his professional staff determine suitable under the circumstances;

4. She will not have access to any passwords or other account information during this protective stay;

5. She cannot leave the residence without the consent of Mr. Puccini;

6. She will be required to wear an ankle bracelet during the stay, preferably waterproof, since Ms. DeBlaine seems always to end up in water somewhere;

7. Liberal access to her attorney will be permitted;
8. Mr. Puccini will be obligated to ensure that Ms. DeBlaine attends all of her scheduled appearances with this Court, including trial.

Rebecca starts arguing with Bruce, whispering "he did this to me," pointing to her shaved head. "He's a monster." The Judge hears portions of Rebecca's dissent and quips, "if you have a problem with that Ms. DeBlaine, I'm sure you would prefer the County's food served in your 8' x 10' cell." She looks shocked at the Judge's remarks. Bruce tells Rebecca, "shut up. This is a great deal. Take it."

Bruce says, "Judge, that is a very good deal! We will gladly take it."

Judge Preston says, "that will be the order of the Court."

CHAPTER THIRTY

Wardrobe Choices

Police Officers Al Williams and Sam Cunningham drive up to Algar's mansion with Rebecca seated in the backseat of the patrol car. Al exclaims looking back at Rebecca, "what a beautiful place. I would give up my home to live here. This is like a Paradise Found." Rebecca makes a smirk on her face. The car swings around a lovely fountain with a Grecian goddess in the center spilling water from an urn. The patrol car comes to rest just steps away from the "triple door" entry causing Sam to comment: "When we came here the last time, it was an emergency that I didn't have time to really concentrate on the magnificence of this stately mansion." Rebecca continues smirking and when the officer turns back around to face the front, Rebecca sticks out her tongue.

She is handcuffed and brought into the atrium of the home with Algar and a corporate attorney present. Officer Al presents Rebecca to them saying, "you are now responsible for the chain of custody of this Defendant" as Al cuts the zip cuffs off of Rebecca. She is wearing the worn and tattered poodle skirt that she was arrested in. With a little humor, Sam smiles and says, "we are delivering her dry this time." Rebecca smirks again. Algar's attorney steps up and says, "we understand the conditions and provisions of the Court's order and we intend to fulfill them in all particulars." The attorney signs a slip of paper acknowledging receipt of Rebecca. "We'll take good care of her," adds the Attorney.

The two officers leave saying, "good day." The attorney instructs Algar, "keep the Court's order by your bedside at all times. If you have any questions, call me or Chet at the office. Once I photo this, I'll send you a copy of the receipt." He shakes Algar's hand and heads for the door.

There is an awkwardness to the presence of the two in the same room. Algar breaks the silences and says, "I bought you three new outfits to wear. There in your closet." Like everything is forgotten, Rebecca chimes in, "really?" Like a little child she goes running up the stairs to see and try them on. When she arrives, she sees the three lone outfits in the closet: one is the Orange prison clothes she has been wearing for the last two weeks; another is a Halloween costume of a black and white convict's outfit with a matching black and white hat; the last one is a red poodle skirt, white blouse with black belt. She looks at the dirty, soiled poodle skirt that she has worn for some time and the new one hanging in the closet. Her temper rises and she races downstairs as fast as when she went up it.

She confronts Algar raising her voice: "You want me to wear the prisoner clothes or the Poodle Skirt. You give me no choice. I won't wear any of them: no prisoner or convict clothes, and, certainly, no 'Poodle Skirt.' What is it with your fetish with Poodle Skirts?" She waits to see what reaction Algar makes. But he makes none. He looks pensive at a statue of Italian origin.

Seeing no reaction, in a huff, she starts to walk away. Algar says, "Rebecca, Baptism." Knowing that it is going to be posted, Rebecca puts on the new Poodle Skirt, Belt and Blouse.

Later that day, a picture of Rebecca soaking wet in the new Poodle skirt and blouse is posted on several media platforms with a caption, "I like this; do you?"

CHAPTER THIRTY-ONE

Terriff's Toll

Assistant Chief Engineer Wade Terriff sits with Seve at a restaurant having lunch discussing the business of the day. Seve introduces the Arc into the conversation saying, "do you think those dual-prefabricated walls would be a benefit to construction?" Terriff says, "That ocean current is strong. Using a barge and slipping them off the back of it may make it difficult to set them in vertical positions." Seve thinks for a moment coming up with an ingenious idea, "if we create the pre-fab walls with 4 feet spacing between them we could achieve sufficient travel lines in the walls." Terriff replies, "then we could bore pathways from one set of walls to the next." "Right," says Seve, "then we can cap the walls at the top, making it possible to add on to the existing walls as the tides rise." Terriff seizes on the important issue, "but the weight of the structure to be laid into ocean is significant. On top of it, how do we have a seamless interlocking system?" Seve ponders the point for a few moments and then answers, "we will use steel rods throughout the connecting walls that interfaced with the adjoining walls and bind them together." Terriff wonders out loud, "do you think that all that boring will create stress fractures in the walls?" Seve responds, "we have to anticipate that there will be stress fractures that may compromise the integrity of the Arc but we can reduce that by pre-boring and plastic cupping bored holes." Terriff answers, "that makes sense. By the time the walls are dropped to the ocean floor, much of the boring will have been completed." "Correct," says smiling Seve.

Changing subjects, "I had an interesting visit from a County investigator named Reed, looking into the death of Monte Enright." "What did he say?" asks Wade. "He wanted to know if I knew anything about his disappearance and then his death." Hearing that, Wade states, "Yes, Reed has scheduled an appointment next week with me to discuss something that he says is County business." "When I met with him I told him we were friends and that we had no disagreements about anything," adds Seve. Just then Wade jumps in and says, "except a little ole project called the Arc." Normally, Wade is a little more diplomatic but for some reason volunteers too much information. He continues, "we wanted the project approved and Monte was the primary hold out. We talked many times about how he could be nullified, his gang of 7 would collapse and the project would be approved." Seve questioningly, "we did?" "Sure, we did. You were so mad you wanted to meet Monte privately and tell him to back off." Seve continues to listen. "One night we were having drinks at the "Loose Goose" and you told me in private whispering you'd love to bash his head in or possibly sabotage his business to keep him, in your words, 'on the straight and narrow.'"

Seve looks at the bottle of liquor on the backside of the bar listening quite intently to what Wade has revealed. Then, Wade whispers to Seve, "we had that strange call from a guy who spoke little English and said he was Russian and that he wanted to speak to you." Seve asks, "do you remember his name?" Wade tries as he can but cannot dredge up the name. Seve attempts to soften the facts and dissuade Wade from going forward with the meeting, "I don't think your facts are well-grounded. Sure, we advocated for the Arc; it was our project. But we certainly would not interfere with the executive process, would we?" Wade sensing that he may have disclosed too much coddles Seve, saying "we were just doing our jobs and we wouldn't force our wills on anyone." Seve agrees, "yes." Wade goes on to add, "I may have the facts a little messed up too." Also agreeing, Seve says, "yes. What you could do is refrain from talking to Reed altogether." Wade replies, "I could but I don't think I can." Just like lightning striking down upon the earth, Wade says, "Peter." "Peter?" Seve queries. "That's the name of the Russian," answers Wade.

Seve goes stone-faced quiet. The lunch ends.

CHAPTER THIRTY-TWO

Squeezed For The Truth

The night was clear with warm trade winds blowing from the East. The Moon was effervescent showing the contours of its seas. The ocean flowed peaceably toward the white sands near Delray Beach. An older home sits couched on a slight bluff looking over the distant waters as a centurion guarding the Palatine Hill. Breaking the peace for a moment, two dark figures appear at one of the back windows of the home facing seaward. They begin to slowly pry it open. They enter the home so cautiously, then noiselessly march up the staircase to the sleeping quarters above. They search the bedrooms and find only one person in bed sleeping. They get on both sides of the bed and place a cloth with chloroform and a struggle ensues. With his hands held down by the one intruder, the other continues to apply the linen over his nares. Eventually, the victim stops fighting and relents into a deep coma. The two men carry the victim downstairs to an ultra-low chest freezer and empty out its contents.

"Yury, why would this guy have such a cold freezer? You don't need it for pizza", tossing it out of the freezer. "Same reason you don't have t-bone steak, Peter," says Yury, flinging the t-bone to the floor. Peter adds, "don't get too friendly with throwing this stuff around, we must have a clean environment here." Yury agrees, "yes. You're right." Once the contents have been emptied, Peter and Yury lift the victim into the deep freeze. Peter comments, "welcome to Iceland." Both laugh and then close the lid. Both men sit on the lid.

"How cold do you think it is inside?" says Yury. I think it drops down to minus 40 degrees," suggests Peter. "That's colder then Smolensk," states Yury. Yury adds, "that means he's got about 15 minutes before he is frozen bacon." Without smiling, Peter changes the subject: "You know this guy was going to mention my name to the County investigator." "Really?" says Yury. "He was going to finger us in the killing of that rig owner," says Peter. Yury laughs and says, "his lips are sealed now." Peter joins in the laughter.

"I have been instructed to make it look like an accident," says Peter. Yury asks, "how do we do that?" "Feed him to the alligators. They need to eat," retorts Peter. "Speaking of eating, put that pizza in the oven and, by the time it is cooked, this guy will be 'frozen tundra.'" Yury unboxes the pizza and slaps it into the oven. As he does so, he asks, "what's the guy's name?" Peter answers, "something like Wade. His last name is used in the import-export business. What is it?" thinks Peter. "Ah yes, it's Terriff. Wade Terriff."

After consuming the pizza, the two men take Wade's frozen, lifeless body to the back of their white van. They say nothing and, given the hour, there are no watchers disturbing their tasks. Yury drives Wade's car behind Peter, as he drives the van down highway 41. Peter pulls the van over when he reaches a suitable place to ditch the body, knowing that it is frequented by a congregation of alligators. With head-mounted flashlights on, they dismount the body from the back of the van and take it down to a stream where snouts of alligators rise from the waterline, lolling, with their tails on the shoreline. Peter and Yury heave the body into the water and the sounds of thrashing and splashing as the alligators go after the fresh, and partially frozen, meat.

Wade's car is parked close to where the consumption takes place. The men drive off in the white van, leaving the Everglades to hold the secret as to Wade's demise.

CHAPTER THIRTY-THREE

Eyeballing the Competition

One night after talking to various doctors, legacy providers and emergency room nurses, Dia receives a strange call. The person on the phone has a hoarse voice and speaks slowly and deliberately, "I need to locate eyes for someone." Dia replies, "that's a difficult order. Corneal implants, yes, but the whole eyeball, that is a big uncertainty. Science has moved in that direction and now eyeball implantation is upon us, but the product is hard to locate. People want their eyes, and sight is such an important sense." The person on the phone says, "I need it for another. A person who is a celebrity and has started developing symptoms of Retinitis Pigmentosa. She needs full vision to perform and dance on stage and can't do that if she can't see out of the corners of her eyes. It started as night vision but now it's full-blown tunnel vision. It's only a matter of time she will be totally blind." Dia listens to what could be a proposal. He continues talking, "she is willing to pay as much as $3 million for one eyeball. She has an ophthalmologist to perform the surgery when a donor eyeball can be located." Holding back a lot of emotion, "$3 million for one eyeball?" inquires Dia. "Yes," says the voice on the phone. Dia immediately disclaims any liability, "if I find the eyeball, you understand there is no guarantee that the eyeball will be fully functioning and the operation will be a success." The voice says, "we know that. But we do not want a cadaver eyeball because certain cells have died and do not regrow. It will have to be fresh." Dia responds like a businesswoman, "I understand. If I provide an eyeball, it will be fresh, but your surgeon has got to transplant immediately." Voice acknowledges the issue, "yes, we have people in place to make that delivery swiftly. He also adds, "we have calls into other organ centers. The one who provides the freshest the fastest will get the $3 million held in trust for this purpose." Dia asks, "is it in trust now?" "Yes, it is," the voice answers. "I'll see what I can do," concludes Dia.

Immediately after the call, she contacts Dr. Ignacio Mendez, who is currently in El Paso at his medical offices. Excited, she announces to Dr. Mendez, "I've got an opportunity of a lifetime. I need one eyeball. If you can locate, I'd be willing to pay $250,000." Dr. Mendez scratching his head, "an eyeball. That's a pretty big order. People on both sides of the fence prize their eyesight. Even to gain entry for their kids is not a reason to go partially blind." Dia says, "time is of the essence. See what you can do."

Hours later, Dr. Mendez calls and tells Dia, "I can't deliver the product. My contacts have all declined and, especially, in Mexico. You are on your own on this one."

The thought has crossed her mind in the past but this time it returns to the surface with a striking counterpoint. Her thoughts happen upon dark and disturbing images. She decides that she wants to avail herself of this opportunity.

It's night and the streets are empty except for homeless people in certain dreadful dark places. Dia thinks, "I was able to perform a surgery on Miserable. It wasn't successful but now if I take one life that is utterly depraved and unfortunate," Dia reasons, "I'm doing a service for the poor lot and, at the same time, for humanity." She travels the streets looking for an ideal specimen. He must fit into a certain demographic she thinks, "he must be in an absolutely pitiful state, addicted to drugs, confused and delusional. He won't know what's missing."

While walking one dark alley, she spies a homeless man sleeping with exposed socks, tattered, revealing a swollen heel, calloused and dirty. He has a long grayish beard and a soiled cap on his head. He's sleeping on newspapers and uses a dirty brown overcoat as a blanket. Dia bends over to see if he awakens and, firstly, if he is breathing. Looking around she thinks, "what an abominable place to live. Wrapped up in filth. With her presence not noticed, she reaches out and nudges him in the shoulder. At first, he doesn't react. She tries again. This time, he coils up into a ball like a sow bug trying to fend off an intruder, yelling "help, help." He settles down when he sees it's a girl about one-third of his age. Startled by his awakening in this fashion, she looks at him, wondering what to say. She somewhat chuckles to herself thinking I've got to ask him, "excuse me for interrupting your sleep, but could I take the last things you own – your body parts and, especially, your eyeball." What then sours her ambition is not his submissive nature, but how clearly he articulated his dilemma: "I have nothing left to give. My shoes were taken two days ago and all my worldly possessions I now wear." His coherent response evokes some sympathy for his plight that even someone as stone-faced as Dia could not ignore. "Sorry," says Dia, and goes to the next alley like she is in the produce section of a grocery store.

The next alley provides a better opportunity. The man is bare-chested and just about to inject himself with heroin. He has brown stubble and appears to be of middle-eastern descent. Not more than 25 or 26 years of age. Just as the full load hits him leaving him on a "high" that he needs to "super charge" now and then, she seizes the opportunity as he falls back on some blankets to enjoy the passage out of this rough life for a moment and approaches him, "I can give you a better high." He doesn't hear her or realize she is present. His life has been tormented by a life riled by demons passing in the night, who care nothing about him just to prey on what's left. She pulls out a hypodermic needle and injects a small amount of propofol. The heroin and the propofol render him totally useless on the verge of death. Realizing this isn't going to pan out well, Dia pulls out a surgeon's scalpel. She had attended some of Dr. Ignacio's operations to learn a little about correct surgical procedure but never used one in a practical setting. She heard that plucking out the eye is not too difficult and it comes out readily. But she has to be careful not to pierce the eye. With very little light she plucks out one and severs its connective tissue. She places the eye into a plastic container. Dia then contemplates her next move. "Do I leave him with one eye should he pull through or assume he will die and go for additional body parts and the last remaining eye?" She determines to leave the other eye in place and she races off into the night not knowing what the fate of the one-eyed homeless man will be.

Later that night, she calls the Voice and announces, "I have the eyeball." Voice says, "good, we'll send for it. I'll be in contact." Voice hangs up.

Dia could not get her mind off of what she had just done. She left a man in the streets taking his eyeball and leaving him in a state close to death. She looks up at Miserable frozen in a position and thinks to herself that may be that will be the end result for the homeless man. She realizes that all of this constitutes a serious criminal act and that to get caught would be the worst ignominy, the shame of her parents. She, too, would be an outcast. Some remorse sets in and is alleviated by the huge payday she will receive.

She waits for the call. The Voice calls back, "meet us at the local airport and we will give you a check and you deliver the eyeball. It will be helicoptered out at that time."

She performs as required and is handed a check for $3 Million and, politely, deposits that into her bank account. In a later conversation, she tells the Voice, "if you need another eyeball give me a call." Once she sees the balance in her bank account, she couldn't help but smile and think, "I've beaten all my competitors to the prize."

CHAPTER THIRTY-FOUR

Dividing the Conquered

Sabrina had observed a slow and somewhat perceptible divide developing between Glen and Jan, as she expected. She thinks, "I've got too much smarts and good looks for them to brush me off. My DTM and denatured balm is my 'nabalm to their souls,' and my introduction to a new luxurious lifestyle. I must be discreet and not set off any alarms. I'll call Jan and get her barometric pressure on the relationship."

She calls and asks, "Hi, Honey, this is Sabrina." Jan laughs and says, "I like my new name." Sabrina surveys, "does he want to say it?" Jan replies, "it took some time but I did what you said, say 'honey is sweeter than spam, Jan.' One night I dressed up incredibly sexy and he was saying 'honey' all night long." He said, "it made him feel like he was dating another." Sabrina asks, "did you feel it was cheating?" "Of course not," is Jan's reply, "it was me he was after." Both laughed at the new excitement introduced in the relationship. Jan adds, "before he felt in charge and his libido was all it could be and would satisfy me every time. No ED or PE." Sabrina interrupts, saying, "that's great." But, as Jan continues, Sabrina realizes a tectonic shift in the relationship, "with the new name, the provocative outfit and my heightened state of arousal, his head has shrunk and withdrawn into its shell." Recognizing the inference, Sabrina states, "sex is fading a bit?" Jan says, "no. It's not existent." Sabrina thinks to herself, "just where I want them to be. I cannot believe it is working out textbook. Let's move to phase three."

Hearing Jan's remarks, Sabrina inquires, "how does that make you feel?" "Good and bad," she exclaims. "I feel good when he looks at me differently but not so good when he can't perform." Sabrina hearing the story says, "Jan, you trust me, right?" Jan states unequivocally, "absolutely, you improved my marriage." Sabrina suggests, "let me talk to Glen over lunch or dinner and see if I can find the source of the problem." Jan exasperated says, "Would you? Could you? I would appreciate it so much." Sabrina says, "tell Glen I will meet him for dinner on Monday, two days before the two of you come in for your weekly massage." Jan says, "Okay." "And," Sabrina suggests, "tell him to pour out his heart and soul to me. Leave no stone unturned." Jan replies, "I will." Sabrina quizzes her, "what are you to say to Glen?" "Have dinner with Sabrina and pour out your heart and soul to her," recites Jan. "That's right," says Sabrina.

That Monday, Sabrina sits at a booth in a very private section of the Screaming Virago Restaurant on a night that guests are infrequent and the place looks like its closed. The owner of the Restaurant offers up intimate dining where curtains can be drawn around partitioned cubicles that surround each booth. The crimson curtains are open from the booth where Sabrina sits and is viewable from the entrance of the Restaurant.

About 7:15 p.m., Glen walks in wearing a tan shirt and black slacks. He sits at the opposite end of the booth on one side and Sabrina sits on the other side. Sabrina believes that Glen is suffering from a cascade of emotions all pointing in her direction. She thinks, "he covets me so much more than that old bag. The slightest little touch will send his lust surging towards me."

She lays the groundwork for the encounter. Sabrina asks, "would you like to order a drink?" Glen says, "a whisky and rye." Sabrina says, "I'll order a lemon drop martini." The waitress comes over and takes their order and steps away. Sabrina breaks the silence and asks, "how do you like the DTM?" Glen smiles and says cloaking his strong desires, "very fulfilling." "Do you have any complaints about the services I perform?" asks Sabrina. Glen laughs, "I wish they were more frequent." Sabrina says, "I can make that happen." "Really?" says Glen. "Of course. Jan loves the new you so much," compliments Sabrina. Causing Glen to say, "she does?" Sabrina says, "yes, she does."

The waitress brings back the drinks and both hold the glasses up and Sabrina says, "lead us in a toast, Glen." Glen tries to think of a good toast and can't, and Sabrina pipes in, "to money for honey." Glen laughs and then looks at Sabrina. "I feel you are so far away from me. Can you move closer to the center of the booth and so will I?" notes Sabrina. They both swing around the booth and end up sitting side by side. When he first approached the booth, he could not see what Sabrina was wearing but now he can. It's a white shift that slings down and barely reaches her thighs. He looks at the shift closely but refrains from making any comments. If he could only salivate, that would indicate his interest in her efforts. Sabrina thinks, "he has stared at my anatomy and it is soaking into his memory banks spilling the saliva over his tongue and lips and causing his sweat glands to release a salty discharge on his forehead." She speaks, "oh, you are sweating. Is it hot in here?" "No," he answers, "I'm fine. I think the whiskey and rye is increasing my heart rate." Sabrina chuckles a bit, "are you sure it's that?"

They order two more drinks and both Sabrina and Glen are getting a little tipsy. After the third go-round, Sabrina asks the waitress to pull the curtain for some intimacy. Glen is left wondering what is going on but does not express any disappointment with the request.

"Glen," says Sabrina, "I was talking to Jan and she wanted me to inquire into a private issue. Are you okay with that?" Glen replies, "I've got nothing to hide. She asked that I pour out my heart and soul to you." Sabrina asks, "Jan wants to know if you are interested in me; it would mean so much to her that you are." "Really?" he says again. "Yes, she wants you to be totally comfortable with me. She thinks I can help with the male thing." Glen not answering but listening. "Let me massage you right here and now." Glen says, "here and now?" Sabrina says, "do you see anyone looking?" Glen looks at the drawn curtains and says, "no."

"Let me do what I do at the salon," as she takes the denatured balm from her purse and starts to massage Glen's neck and back. The effect is almost instantaneous. The interaction of the whiskey and rye with the balm places Glen in a semi-conscious state of suggestion. In about 10 minutes, he is totally under Sabrina's spell. "You want me so bad. You forget you are married and believe that you are single. You feel at home here and that your wife is watching. You want to take your hands and start massaging me. I need a massage badly. No one ever massages good ole Sabrina. You have no other thought than to massage Sabrina." To encourage him to the next step, she guides his hands on to her breasts and then to her thighs. He starts groping and massaging, feeling Sabrina out. Sabrina croons, "that makes me feel good. You smell my perfume and you like it as a bee to honey. You want to pollinate the flower to get the honey." Glen is totally absorbed in the sexcapade and his hands are going everywhere. "Touch me there if you can?" Glen goes down into the private area, causing Sabrina to react.

Sabrina thinks, "now the coup de grace." "Glen, can I sit on your lap?" Glen nods his head. Sabrina sits on his lap and undulates softly. Suddenly, Glen hardens and Sabrina notes it, "well done, Glen." She kisses Glen and Glen kisses back. Sabrina in and up and down motion says, "say you love me." Glen hesitates, but with the influence of the balm, the DTM and the alcohol, it doesn't take long before he says, "I love you, I love you." "Good, Glen, keep saying it until you believe it," says Sabrina. Glen continues saying it, "I love you, I love you, I love you." Sabrina continues the mind control by saying, "You love me more than Jan. Jan is just Honey, looking to take your money. Go ahead, Glen, repeat after me. 'I love you more than Jan. Jan is just Honey, looking to take your money.' Repeat it again." Glen repeats at least 10 times.

The session ends after Glen waits up 1 hour later. Glen and Sabrina kiss and hold hands as they exit the restaurant. Glen that night sleeps in another bedroom from Jan.

CHAPTER THIRTY-FIVE

Programming to Kill

Tyesha never used her skills and talents in a minacious way but the mentation grew from a sprout of devious control into something bigger, changing in size and scope and channeling from a portal that should never have been opened. The more she pondered the subject, the more it became defined and transparent. She was going to program to kill. Her subject was Prosperity; her target was Meghan. She had to devise a failsafe, fools proof plot that will bring down the very foundations of Meghan Middlebrook.

"I need to make this swift and divisive, leaving no trace, encrypting the program to delete itself within a 72-hour period," she thinks. She wonders, "will that be enough time to indoctrinate Prosperity to act? The mind's sensitivity varies from person to person. The difference here is a criminal act. Can I suggest to someone to commit a criminal act?" Thinking out loud, "I read somewhere that there was significant subliminal messaging and brainwashing with the Massacre at Jonestown and Patty Hearst and the Symbionese Liberation Army, but those events were not based solely on messaging but a certain level of coercion to make them succeed. Here, there is only subliminal suggestion that may arouse enough of an acidic reflex to cause a violent end."

That night, Tyesha types the lethal program that will encourage Prosperity to do the unthinkable flagitious act. She starts with subtle clues. The introductory video shows a girl staring deeply into a mirror wearing a black cocktail dress and a black feathered hat. Hypnotized by the trance, she sees another woman, M&M, caustically reprimanding her shouting directly into her ear. The girl starts to cry and red blood pours out of the girl's eyes rolling down her face and neck. The streams of blood keep pouring as long as the woman yells into the girl's ear. Finally, the girl grabs a dagger and stabs the woman, who falls to the ground, and the girl's face is restored to its former beauty and the girl smiles at what she has done. Tyesha completes the program way into the quiet hours of the night and encrypts it to destroy itself within 72 hours.

The next day, Tyesha delivers the program and downloads to Prosperity's computer. Prosperity walks by Tyesha's station and asks, "is it in?" Tyesha answers, "yes. Ready for you." "Thank you," Prosperity says, planting a kiss on Tyesha's cheek. She arrives at her workstation and sits down to enjoy the latest economic quiz program. Not long after, she is totally absorbed into the program receiving the tranche of information through flashpoint technology.

Unlike the past, this program is time sensitive with an expiration date of now 65 hours. Tyesha hopes that the results will be promising. "I wish I could know what is going on in her mind," Tyesha thinks. "Is she realizing that the flashpoints are clearly insisting upon the commission of a criminal act, which would make her aware that I was trying to use her to kill Meghan? Or, is it something more innocuous, like the casual suggestion of some general theme of injuring another?" The only solace Tyesha can grasp is from past experiences when Prosperity has followed the flashpoint tranche of information in the way it was programmed. The only thing I can do now is wait and see," she thinks.

Still irritated by her with Prosperity, Meghan determines to confront Tyesha directly. "With all your clever suggestions and manipulations, don't get too attached to your probation evaluation," says Meghan directly to Tyesha. "Why," says Tyesha. "Because we don't allow probation evaluations to act as promotional opportunities," states curtly Meghan. She adds, "so, you are aware, it is my intent to form a panel of Senior Economists within one week to override your promotion to Senior Economist. Just be thankful you passed your probation as a Junior Economic Consultant."

Hearing the interaction, Prosperity runs over to Tyesha's station and says, "get out of here, you bitch," directing her venom toward Meghan. "This is my employee and I supervise her. You don't. Stay out of my business." Some of the morning's messaging had some effect on Prosperity who starts to push Meghan away and Tyesha's hand goes up between the two women and Meghan leaves the area without any scuffle.

Tyesha thinks, "this encounter may have more far-reaching implications in delivering the message because physical interactions mixed with programming may nudge the hypnotic suggestion into a "real world" perception enhancing the result.

Prosperity sits at the program day and night, leaving only to eat and use the restroom. Tyesha paces back and forth at her desk keeping track of the time, saying, "40, 39, 38 hours." At the 24 hour mark, almost 2 full days into sitting at her station, Prosperity runs up to Tyesha and says, placing her hands on her butt, "you are so important to me and my life. You have made me a changed woman and I appreciate what you have done. No one is going to stand in the way of your advancement." Then, Tyesha hears the words she thought she never would hear, "I hate Meghan with all my heart and soul." Tyesha plays into the suggestion by stating, "you have given your entire career to McElroy working around the clock to advance its objectives, only to have your decisions countermanded and rejected by a less senior employee. What are you going to do about it?" asks Tyesha. Prosperity answers, "I'll do something but first I need to get back to my computer." "Sure," says Tyesha.

CHAPTER THIRTY-SIX

Done Did Deed

For the next 12 hours Prosperity studies the screen and the flashpoints with a certain religiosity like a nun to morning prayers. When Tyesha, looking great in a black tights and a red rose in her hair, comes to work, she sees the flashing of the screen at Prosperity's workstation and knows she's been at it all night. She decides to approach her. "Hi," says Tyesha, startling Prosperity in a trance-like state. Prosperity's eyes appear afloat in the eye socket like she is unable to focus. Tyesha asks, "are you alright. Why are your eyes floating?" With that Prosperity's eyes focus on Tyesha's facial features. Hesitating a bit, Prosperity exclaims out loud, "we're twin sisters. I am going to wear that same outfit today, including the red rose." She gets up and hugs Tyesha, again placing her hands on her derriere and this time squeezing it very hard.

Prosperity states excitedly, "I know how I'm going to do it." Tyesha reading between the lines says, "surprise me." Prosperity continues, "you know that economic summit taking place at the Cosmos downtown, are you going?" "Tyesha answers, "I have not signed on for it but I may go." Prosperity proclaims, "she is going." Tyesha raises a finger over her lips to silence any identification of who "she is." She giggles and says, "I'll track her down like an old English Foxhound." Tyesha smiles causing her to ask, "when?" "After the summit, it happens," sniggers Prosperity. "So, you will be there?" questions Tyesha. "Only in the darkest outreaches of the summit," is Prosperity's reply.

Something unusual has taken hold of Tyesha. Normally, a health nut who eats her fair share of salads and a solid vegan diet, tonight is different. She has this craving to eat red meat and it is all-compelling. She goes to the store after work and buys a rump roast. She comes home and sets the roast on a wood cutting block. With a carving knife she repeatedly stabs the meat, over and over again. Some of the blood from the meat sprays up into her face, but she continues to stab it repeatedly. The meat is looking more and more tattered and Tyesha hyperventilates as she continues to thrust the knife in and out of the roast. Like on the verge of an orgasmic rapture, she scurries over to the condiment section and grabs taco sauce and a ketchup bottle and pours all the contents on the meat. She continues hacking away at the meat with more and more blood, sauce and ketchup spraying all over her face. She looks in the mirror and seeing her face almost completely covered with blood and sauce, she smiles and refuses to wipe it off. She pulls out of her purse the brightest red lipstick she possesses and applies it to her lips with a thick application. She re-looks at herself in the mirror and then nosedives into the meat like a vulture clawing upon some recently killed carrion on a hot asphalt surface, burning in the desert sun. She grabs the raw meat in her teeth and rips at the roast, chews it and swallows. She dives down again for a second bite. Grabbing her hand mirror, she looks as she rips the meat from the roast and holds it in her teeth smiling at the sight.

That night Prosperity sits on a bus bench across the street from the economic summit at the Cosmos Downtown. It is after 10 p.m. and the conference is over. She watches Meghan exit the summit with another economist heading over to Tom's Tavern next door. Meghan sneaks up and looks through the window to see the male economist and Meghan sharing some sliders and scotch. They both are deep in conversation. True to her word, Prosperity is wearing black tights with a red rose in her hair. Her lips are pasted with red lipstick. Prosperity wonders, "how long are they going to chit-chat?" She goes to the front door and sees that the place closes at 10:30 p.m.

She waits until that time. It is 10:35 p.m., and Meghan and the male economist are the last to leave Tom's Tavern. As they exit the establishment, the owner is heard to say, "Thanks for coming." Meghan and the economist part company at the door and Meghan must trek through the back alley to the parking pavilion for the Cosmos Downtown.

After leaving the fellow economist, Meghan looks up at the sky and sees some low-flying clouds move across a crescent moon blotting it out of the sky altogether. The alley is damp and wet from a recent rain and, as she walks, she hears water running off of a gutter on to an open section of the alley. She avoids the spill water and looks at the approaching pavilion for lighted security. She wonders, "why wouldn't they light this section of the alley given its proximity to the Hotel?" The only answer she hears elicits from her mouth, "because they are too cheap to install one." She hears a clanging on a waste disposal bin from behind her and she looks around quickly. It is too dark to see. She thinks out loud, "it's probably a worker at Tom's Tavern throwing away the night's refuse." Nonetheless, she decides to quicken her step. Suddenly, she sees a black creepy crawler approach her with a black ski mask, startling Meghan and stopping her advance toward the pavilion. Meghan begins to back up as the dark creature moves closer and closer to her. The creature raises a dark knife ready to plunge into Meghan and holding it over her head ready to knife the defenseless Meghan. Suddenly, she exasperates, "I can't do this," lowering the knife and beginning to walk away.

Then, from behind, coming from a secret hiding place near the waste disposal bin, another black-tight creature with a rose in her hair wearing a frontal ski mask, rushes from behind and says, "this is how you do it," hacking away at Meghan from her backside and, when she falls, her frontside, repeatedly striking with the knife 30-40 times. Seeing all of this the first dark creature runs off frightened and intimidated at the sight of the killing. Hearing the screams then death cries of Meghan, a parking pavilion man wrestles the second creature to the ground and holds it until the authorities arrived.

The scene is taped off and the dark creature is carted off in a patrol car. Before she enters the patrol car, her frontal mask is removed. It is Tyesha.

Little did this programmer know that to create the program and to review it for its use by others, makes that programmer fall victim to its subliminal messages and, ultimately, its flashpoints as well.

CHAPTER THIRTY-SEVEN

Brainwasher's Self-Defense

Ranger Sprinkles works as an investigative reporter for the Salem World Gazette at its offices in Salem, Oregon. He graduated from Oregon State University in Journalism at Corvallis, interning at Salem World Gazette through his last two years there. Though he protects the right of press religiously, he is open for assuring his success in the field by networking whenever the opportunity arises. If that means he applies the source privilege loosely to get at a story or influence a contact, he will. The story supersedes any privilege as long as it does not adduce to malice. Today, he stumbles upon an online article out of New York. He views the title of the article, "Brainwasher asserts self-defense over program she created."

Intrigue with the article he reads that a young girl in her 20's named Tyesha Biggerstaff created a software program to subliminally control her manager to kill another manager. He reads that the program backfired when the brainwasher became the brainwashed. When the manager refused to kill the other manager, Tyesha knifed the manager to death. He examines her picture and finds her strikingly beautiful, yet he thinks to himself, "why would anyone with her beauty do such a terrible deed?"

Ranger investigates further after reading the article. Once he sees that she graduated from Dartmouth, mastered at Stanford

University and received a doctorate from Harvard, all in Economics, he races over to the Editor-in-Chief and tells him about the storyline. "Stan," says Ranger, "I found a story that people will love. A young girl attempts to program another to kill her boss, but the program backfires with the other refusing to kill but the programmer is herself brainwashed and she kills her boss." Stanley Grinstein, the Editor of the Salem World Gazette, exclaims, "what a story. Get more fill on it and we'll put in on our front page."

Ranger calls up his Portland contact Harry Berger. "I have a story for you, Harry," says Ranger. "What," says Harry. Ranger explains the story in detail and asks, "since you have done CSI, what should I do? The girl is magnificent!" Harry queries, "what do you mean 'Magnificent?'" "She's beautiful, young and smart as a whip," answers Ranger. Harry furthers the inquiry, "how young?" "Not more than 25 years," replies Ranger. Harry astounded, "not more than 25 years."

Thinking for a moment, he tells Ranger, "I came upon a similar story out of Ft. Worth, where a Texas U. engineer blew up his competitor's building. The guy was brilliant and good-looking." He adds, "these are unusual times but what's with all these attractive people going criminal. Is it coincidence? Or, is there some hidden reason for it happening now?" Harry informs Ranger, "you should check deeper into the individuals to ascertain if their early development had some effect on their criminal misbehavior." Ranger concludes, "thanks for the information, I'll check into their personal lives."

That day, Ranger calls Ft. Worth Star Telegram and speaks to the writer of the article on Dirk Rainjoy. "Hi, Herman, this is Ranger at the World Gazette out of Salem, Oregon. I wanted to get some information on the Dirk Rainjoy case." Herman asks, "what would you like to know?" Ranger rhetorically asks, "why would someone of this guy's brilliance and Adonis looks blow up his competition?" Herman answers, "we don't know. We did a full exposition on the guy, including the prosecution of the case. Couldn't figure it out. Neither could the lead prosecutor. The guy pleads guilty without a trial defense. We really don't know what was going on in his mind." "Do you have any information about this guy's upbringing?" asks Ranger. Herman states, "I have a biographical profile on him that may be helpful. But that's probably all we have now. His company folded after all the lawsuits filed by investors. Most of the information has been shredded or locked in a vault somewhere that no one can get at. I'll send over the profile today." Ranger terminates the conversation with "thank you."

After getting the biographical information on Tyesha from the McElroy Management's website, Ranger compares the detailed information on Dirk with Tyesha. Tyesha's resume shows that she was "genetically shaped," but Dirk only reads "EGG."

Unsure of what EGG means, he does some research online trying to discover its meaning. Ranger asks a co-worker, Hazel, "what do you think EGG means?" She ponders the question for a moment, then suggests, "maybe it has something to do with impregnation – the egg and the sperm." Ranger is quick to nullify that answer by saying, "why would a person put that on his resume?" Hazel then gives the hint that causes the implosion, "because, because he wants to advertise he has talents above the normal individual – like a superman." Ranger ruminates on that thought and pointing upward, "you hit on something, Hazel." She smiles back and he races off to a news library.

He finds in the World Gazette library, a relic of information that is 24 years old, written by one of the journalists at the Gazette, "a new technology allows for 'gene precreation.'" He looks at the title of the article and repeats, "gene precreation?" Not gene procreation." He reads further that "a company called Enbryo is bringing a new and magical process to baby-making that allows for the couple to choose the traits and characteristics their baby will have." He further reads, "the technology scoots the genes in the direction that best suits the parents' wants and desires, such as intelligence, good looks, and freedom from certain anomalies and illnesses."

The article then states, "this is the wave of the future and Enbryo Genetic Guidance is positioning itself to be in the forefront of genetic shaping." With that Ranger lifts his head and says out loud, "EGG is Enbryo Genetic Guidance."

Ranger contacts Enbyro and is directed to Dr. Marjorie Birmbaum. After identifying herself, Ranger announces, "I am a reporter from the Salem World Gazette and want to inquire as to what Enbryo's response is to the Tyesha Biggerstaff murder." Marjorie states, "we are familiar with the case but we have nothing to do with it." "But her resume identifies her as being genetically shaped by your company," he argues. "What does genetic shaping have to do with someone's killing?" answering him rhetorically. She adds, "genetically shaping only sets up parameters for gene suggestion for certain traits and characteristics. It does not make someone a killer. Look, if I gene-shape you to have blue eyes instead of brown, how does that make you a criminal or killer? It doesn't. Blue eyes, brown eyes, gray eyes, hazel eyes are not determining traits for a murderer. They are just the color of one's eyes." After the speech, Ranger inquires, "has Enbryo conducted any studies on genetic shaping and criminal behavior?" She answers, "no. There is no rhyme or reason to conduct a study on traits that have no realistic relationship to criminal behavior." Ranger concludes and says, "thank you for Enbyro's position on the subject."

Several days later, the Salem World Gazette releases its article on the Tyesha Biggerstaff case and, as expected, the article zooms across its readership with a craving addiction for more news on the subject.

Evelyn Wattig reads the article and reaches out to Ranger. "Hi,

I'm Evelyn Wattig and I read your article on the Biggerstaff case. Do you think there is a genetic reason for the murder?" Ranger answers, "It's a big leap of faith to tie a gene-shaped individual into a murderer. How does a gene make a person a slayer? The criminal chromosome was debunked years ago?" Evelyn explains, "my son was genetically shaped and did things to our cat that were unimaginable. He refused to go to counseling and mysteriously our cat died one day. Do you think there is a connection?" Ranger defaults to the reporter position, "I just can't print speculation in a news article; otherwise, I may be acting with malice. I have to have a concrete basis for the things I put in newsprint." Evelyn then questions, "is that the reason you left out genetic shaping in the article?" "Yes," he answers, "the only reason." "Okay," says Evelyn, then she ends the call.

Evelyn turns her attention to Enbryo and calls Marjorie Birmbaum directly. Mad and, at the same time, bewildered, she tells Marjorie, "my son killed the cat and this Tyesha girl is up on murder charges. What are you going to do about it?" Feeling she is being remonstrated, Dr. Birmbaum lashes out: "I don't have to do a thing. We shape genes to please our customers. They are all satisfied. Just because your child killed the family cat is not something we are responsible for. You raised the child and there was some influence in the home that caused him to do that. Don't blame us." Disgusted Evelyn hangs up on "don't blame us."

After the call with Ranger and then Evelyn, Dr. Birmbaum contacts Enbryo's Research and Development Department and suggests that the company do a limited number of brain and body scans on recently gene-shaped children. She adds, "this research is to be done for my eyes only and that the costs for the scans will be paid for by Enbryo."

CHAPTER THIRTY-EIGHT

Mental Observation

Discipline has been stepped up for violations of house rules. Rebecca not only has to immerse herself in water to cleanse any impurity of wrongdoing but now she has to stand in a corner near the cherry-wooded library striking her hind with a switch gently. Her hair is slowly growing out, now about 1 quarter inch of stubble. She hates this discipline with anger and moments of despair. She whispers to herself and looking around that he is not present, "I am just a pawn in this crazy child's world of fantasy. Sometimes he incorporates me into the video game, requiring that I act out scenes that he sees depicted on the screen. One time he wanted me to bark like a sheep dog, when I refused I spanked myself as punishment. I've had it with this troubled youth."

When her time in the corner is up, she goes up stairs and passes the boy descending the stairs, who states: "remember to wear the prison clothes." She answers somewhat defiantly, "yes sir." She dresses in the prison clothes and comes downstairs. She sees Algar playing a video game on a finely ornate white couch. As she passes she says, "I'll make you lunch," hesitating a moment and then adding, "sir." She proceeds into the kitchen where she plots revenge. She glances at her image in a shiny hanging pot in the center of the wooden island of that kitchen. She says, "I look hideous – shaved head, prison clothes and a face unaccentuated by any makeup, powder or eyeliner. Two can play this game," walking over to the swinging kitchen door and seeing Algar with his back to her on a video game. She goes over to a wood block and cuts some luncheon meat to serve as a sandwich. She adds condiments and mayonnaise, then, looks up and around to see that no one is watching. Grabbing a container that holds a substance similar to thallium, she pours a little on the meat. Then, she thinks of the retribution and disgrace she has experienced and, overcome with animosity for that treatment, she pours more onto the meat and looking up in hushed tones speaks, "if this results in your end, I'll be happy." She places the sandwich, milk and cookies on a tray and walks toward the kitchen door with a chuckle.

Unbeknownst to Rebecca, the house, since her arrest, has been outfitted with cameras secreted away in compartments, objects of art, clocks and security systems. The camera system has been downloaded on his computer so with a click of a button he can go from playing a video game to watching Rebecca throughout the house, including the bathrooms. When she went into the kitchen, he clicked on the camera system to see what she was doing. He saw and heard what she said.

She presents the meal to Algar, "here's your lunch, sir." "Thanks," says Algar. He continues, "I want you to eat it." "No, I can't do that. I made it for you, sir," she answers. He demands, "eat it now," with his voice rising. She retorts, "I can't. I'm not hungry. My stomach doesn't feel well." He orders, "eat it now, or I'm going to send the police over." "I really can't," she renews. "Is there something wrong with it?" questions Algar. "No," she replies. "Then, eat it now," the boy exclaims. With great hesitation, Rebecca places the sandwich in her mouth and slowly eats the first bite. "More," says the boy. Rebecca eats another bite and chews it slowly. After the third bite, she grasps her stomach and falls to the floor.

The boy calls his corporate representative and tells him, "Rebecca tried to kill herself." The representative named Shaffer says, "oh, no, this is not going so well. She may have to be under a 72- hour observation period. We will so inform the court."

Later, that day the ambulance takes the unconscious Rebecca to the hospital and, after her stomach is pumped, she is taken to a mental hospital for observation.

Shaffer speaks to the Psychiatrist on duty at Metro Psychological Facility, "she is in a very depressive state. Here are some videos taken today and, at other times, at the home showing her in a corner, soaking wet, striking herself with a switch. She apparently placed poison on a sandwich, which she ate to end her life. Here is the video of her in the kitchen wherein she states: "if this results in your end, I'll be happy." She was talking to herself in the kitchen. As you know, she is up on embezzlement charges and resisting arrest. Only, by the grace of God, did the boy intervene and agree to protective custody over her and in her fragile state to spare her from spending time in jail. I have consulted with the boy, Algar, and he believes, as I do, that Rebecca would benefit from electroconvulsive shock therapy (ECT) to snap her out of this depressive state." "Thank you for the information," says Psychiatrist Malvory. "Usually, we need the consent of the family, but, in the absence of the family and the fact that we have a protective custody order, we can follow the suggestions of you and the boy provided you give your consent for the treatment." Shaffer answers, "we both give our consent to the procedure."

One day later, Rebecca is lying on a bed at Metro Psychological Facility and is tied down as she vehemently protests the administration of the ECT. They put a block in her mouth so she doesn't bite her tongue. Her speech is garbled. The shock treatment is administered with Rebecca's head vibrating with the passage of shock through her brain and body. After the shock treatment, she lies motionless on the bed. The straps in place are removed and she is taken back to her room.

For the next day or so, she is confused, tired and has suffered some loss of memory, forgetting things like the current year and her age. She has experienced some regression formation, thinking that she is a young girl. She keeps asking, "where's my mom?" The staff answers, "we don't know."

Later, she is released back into the care of Algar and returned to the mansion. A caretaker dresses her in the Halloween costume still remaining in her closet. The hospital sends a report to the Court that Rebecca has attempted suicide and underwent a successful ECT.

After the video was posted of Rebecca standing in a corner soaking wet striking herself, the video of her dressed in a Halloween costume is also posted online. Both viewed together shows a girl with serious mental problems.

CHAPTER THIRTY-NINE

Hatchet Job

It was on a small hill that rises above the river that death intersects with life. He didn't know what had hit him. He was a good man who fell on sour times and was swallowed up into a recent life of inebriation. The townspeople did not sympathize with the sudden change in his fate from an insurance salesman to a reprobate in the matter of a few months. He overspent to keep those he thought loved him financially secure; that was his only sin. A sin that no one found exemplary now since he had become a burden on society. Without the financial means, those loved ones moved on to greener pastures leaving him to wallow in pauperism. For Ted, life was unfair and the push of the townspeople to move him out of town was unjust. The initial suggestion by those in government was to find another home. But, as the months passed, it was law enforcement that physically shoved him out of town. He built a small little encampment on the outskirts of town made from birch tree branches and plastic sheeting. Though it was not Nirvana, it had the semblance of stability in his world and he began to feel safe there. One night his sleep was interrupted by a man dressed in black with a pointed chin and pale white face. He was hunched over looking at Ted while he slept. He mumbled something like, "you dead? I can take you to the horizon where life ends and death begins." That night put fear in Ted and he grabs a walking stick and braces it over his resting body like he is prepared to defend himself and his makeshift homestead. Seeing the stick, the dark prominent creature walks away into the darkness.

Days pass and Ted begins to think it was a fluke or, even something rarer, a specter. He lays his stick some distance away from his sleeping quarters and feels at ease with his security. That night, he guzzles too much whiskey and is desensitized to pain.

It is a starlit night and Orion's belt could be plainly seen from the northern sky. While in his drunken stupor, a needle prick penetrates his buttocks and he exhibits no signs of discomfort or pain. A tall female with black hair whispers to a voice in the distance, "he's out like a light." She pulls out a pocket flashlight and shines it on the torn grungy pants that Ted wears. She then grabs a scalpel and begins to cut at the pants while Ted sleeps unaware of what's happening. Once the pants are completely cut and removed, the tall female flashes the light on his backside. The flash reveals the green-yellowish eyes of the female. She wears a brown beret and works diligently without making a sound. All that can be heard are the cutting strokes against the cotton shirt. As she removes the shirt from the body, she holds it up and comments with one word, "nasty," as she flings it to the ground as if it were a scorpion ready to bite. Sensing the cold and hearing the word "nasty," Ted begins to move. He looks up at the two dark figures and screams. His legs have been anesthetized by some narcotic and he reacts, "my legs. What's wrong with my legs?" He reaches down to touch them and looks up at the creatures hovering over him. He tries to crawl with his hands and slowly moves upslope like a caterpillar with a few legs missing. The mysterious people follow behind him for some distance. His naked body creeping on the ground with much difficulty. Realizing that he cannot out crawl his captors who follow some length behind, he speaks unclearly and in garbled tones, "please, leave me alone. I have nothing to give. I'm broke and poor." The female voice sums up, "put an end to this."

Without saying a word, a hatchet comes down upon the left arm severing it from the shoulder. Ted screams in complete agony, "help me. Someone help me. Don't do this to me." The hatchet falls again splitting the right arm from the shoulder socket. Ted lies there unable to move his legs with arms gone. He is stopped dead in his tracks. Realizing the end is coming, he pleads for his life. "I have nothing to give you. Don't kill me." The female pulls his hair yanking it backward so it lifts his head and whispers in his ear, "you have a wealth of organs that can be harvested." She injects the needle into the back of his neck. Moments later, Ted stops breathing.

The female directs the other creature, "cut his legs off and I'll take care of the delicate stuff." Within the matter of one hour, the organs and body parts have been taken and placed in plastic containers not far from where the operation took place.

Later, that night, a boat was heading down river to the Trafalgar Bridge where a sack containing Ted was being deposited into the slimy goo.

CHAPTER FORTY

Questioning

Deputy Sheriff Jason Lazenby sits across the table in an interview room facing Seve Aguado. "I asked you to come in this morning for questioning regarding the disappearance of Wade Terriff. It is more discreet here than the County offices. I hope you understand," says Jason. "I sure do," says Seve. Jason continues, "there is a missing person's report for Wade Terriff and we have been investigating it for some time. We found his car on highway 41 and footprints were taken not far from the car on a ridge just above a stream where alligators inhabit. By the time we found the car, if Wade was an alligator's stew, there would be little trace of evidence except DNA in its excrement. We haven't found that excrement. We are left with the break in the home. Other than prying through the window and an ensuing struggle in Wade's bed, the only thing we have to go on at the moment is shoe prints. There was no blood left at the scene. I have some information that you and Wade had lunch shortly before his disappearance. Is that right?" Seve answers coldly, "yes." "May I ask what you talked about?" says Jason. Carefully phrasing his words, Seve states, "we were talking business," looking around at the two-way mirror. "He was your assistant and collaborator in developing and obtaining funding for the Arc of Tranquility, is that right?" inquires Jason. "Yes," Seve bluntly answers. "Did you two have any disagreements over the project?" asks Jason. "None," is Seve's reply. "When was the last time you saw Wade?" Seve answers, "that day at lunch." "So, he disappeared sometime after lunch and the following workday," concludes Jason. "That I don't know the answer. We had lunch. Lunch ended and we went our own ways," comments Seve. "During lunch, did Wade tell you anything that would cause you to be concerned about his safety?" Jason asks. "No. He lives alone and he never mentioned any problems in his personal life. He seemed happy with home life as he was with work life," mentions Seve. "Have you ever been to his house?" asks Jason. "Yes. On one or two occasions," quips Seve. "Was there anything unusual about the house?" Seve replies, "not that I remember." "This is a personal question: do you know if he slept with no clothes on?" Seve answers somewhat indignantly, "that is far too personal for me to know the answer." "Sorry, but we haven't found any clothing at the scene of the struggle or the site of where his car is located," explains Jason.

After getting the limited answers from Seve to his questions, Jason leans back in his wood swivel chair and looks Seve over for any clues that might betray his earlier statements. He then smiles and says, "Monte Enright died under disturbing circumstances. Would you call him an 'antagonist' to the passage of the Arc of Tranquility?" Seve answers quickly, "No. I deal with projects all the time and commissioners regularly dissent on my projects and I harbor no bitterness toward them. It is how business is done here in Miami." Jason then digs in, "wouldn't you say the 'Arc of Tranquility' project was your pet project? That if it succeeded you would be a nationwide celebrity?" Seve counters, "yes, the Arc is a pet project and, yes, I could garner a lot of attention off a successful project like that. But I would never go so far as to commit criminal acts to see it succeed. That's simply not my nature or prerogative." "Do you have any idea who would be behind the disappearance of Wade Terriff?" Seve replies, "I really don't." Hesitating a moment and then he adds, "we had some enemies on the project that would like to see the project doomed and defeated. There is no telling what steps they would take to stop the project from going forward."

"That's interesting to hear," says Jason, playing along with the accusation, "who were the enemies?" Realizing he stepped on a subject, he shouldn't have volunteered, Seve says generically, "anytime you have a project, there are people who oppose it, politically, or for other reasons. I cannot name any of the enemies but I had my car 'keyed' one night when I went to a restaurant." Then, out of left field, "did the keying take place at the 'Loose Goose?'" asks Jason. Seve jolts a little with that appellation but he maintains his coolness. Trying to cover up the keyed incident, "I really don't remember. It was some time back though." Jason then furthers the inquiry, "do you know George, the owner and bartender of the Loose Goose?" "No, I did not make his acquaintance," replies Seve. "He told me that he was definitely opposed to the Arc because it was too expensive and he'd hoped the flooding would have reduced his shoreline competition. I guess he was an Arc enemy," Jason laughing over the play of words. "I didn't know that," retorts Seve. Seve's forehead begins to wet with perspiration. "Have you ever had dinner at the Loose Goose? I hear the food is really good," asks Jason. Realizing that Jason is circling like a vulture, Seve cannot evade the questions with unspecific answers. He states, "I may have been there once or twice." "Thinking on it a little more, do you think you got your car keyed at the Loose Goose?" states Jason. Inside Seve is crumbling. He thinks, "he's caught me red-handed. He must know something that the keying took place at the Loose Goose. If I dodge the question, he will catch me in a lie and I'll be a suspect in the killing of Monte. Should I request an attorney? What do I do? If I get up and run, I'll be painted as the killer. Where do I run? I'm at the police station." Seve blurts out, "now, that I think about it, I believe the keying took place at the Loose Goose." "Did you ever find out, who killed your car?" asks Jason. "Hearing the missed verb, "you mean "keyed" right?" responds Seve. Jason stumbling with his words, "I'm sorry, yes, keyed your car?" Seve answers, "no."

Seve is going into a panic. "He used the word 'killed' rather than 'keyed,' he must be thinking of me as a suspect. What do I do?" The interview continues, "do you know if you had dinner with anyone the night your car was keyed?" Seve answers, "I don't believe so," thinking it would be better to punt the answer then commit to a story line. Then, the loaded shotgun question is posited, "George told me he saw you with Wade the night your car was keyed. He said that you came into the Loose Goose after finding your car was keyed asking for reparations." "I think that did happen," states Seve. "So, Wade was there the night your car was keyed?" "I don't remember for sure, but that may be the case," Seve is coming unglued. He is being pigeon-holed into responses and there is no escaping the interview. He thinks, "he is going to ask the next question that will incriminate me to the point I will have no way out. I need to terminate the meeting."

Seve says, "I really have to go. I have another commitment I need to attend to." Surprisingly, Jason answers, "sure, this is not a custodial investigation. It's just an interview. You are free to leave." Seve says, "okay," and walks out the door. He thinks, "next time, there is any meeting, I'm going to have one, if not, two attorneys by my side."

CHAPTER FORTY-ONE

Honey Needs Money

Jan calls Sabrina about the quick changing circumstances at her home. "Sabrina, I don't know what's happened to Glen. He seldom talks to me. He doesn't even want to do the joint massages anymore. I'm really concerned." Sabrina assuages the situation saying, "it can't be that bad. You know how men are. One moment, they're interested in sex; the next moment they want to play golf. Be patient. Can you come for a massage today?" Jan feeling the pressure of isolation and distance in the home responds, "yes, I can come now." "I'll be waiting for you," answers Sabrina.

Sabrina has reached a delicate point in breaking the ties that bind. Too much of a shove in one direction may cause a violent reaction where Sabrina is fingered as the intermeddler – the culprit who is destroying the marriage. She thinks, "I must act gingerly not to disturb the suspicions directed between Glen and Jan so they won't be misdirected to me. I need a failsafe approach. She thinks on it.

Shortly, Jan comes through the door with difficulty. A lot of the DTM has worn off. Jan seems confused and disoriented with the breakdown in the marital accord. Before her steps were somewhat vibrant and sure, now they are feeble and weak. She moves toward Sabrina, who she views as a Shaman or a spiritual leader of sorts, that has worthy advise. "Good morning, Jan," as Sabrina greets Jan. They embrace but it is not the warm hug in the past; it's now like a shoe that has been disconnected from the sole with the sole slapping along the ground. It needs to be sewn back together. Jan says, "Not good. I'm dizzy." Sabrina says, "here, lie on the table." Jan's clothes drop off with no hesitation as if the load is too much to bear. Jan gets up on the table and lies face down. Sabrina asks, "towel?" "No," is Jan's smothered reply.

While lying face down, Sabrina chooses the right weapons to influence. The denatured balm comes out and is rubbed over the backside, legs and buttocks. The massage is having some effect on Jan before Sabrina speaks. She asks, "would you like a stiff one?" Jan seems lost in the DTM. Sabrina says something most unusual when she hears no response from Jan, "I'm going to give you an injection of straight whisky. It should help you feel better." Sabrina is not sure what the interaction of the denatured balm and the whisky will have, but says to herself, "It will relax her more to the suggestions I will make." Almost instantaneously, Jan sounds drunk, making sounds of belching from a couple of orifices. Whispering in her ear, "let's help you turn over." With Sabrina's help, Jan turns over. She continues her suggestions, "he doesn't love you anymore. You want more. You want someone younger. Say it with me, 'I want more. I want more. I want more.' Go ahead and repeat." Jan, in a hypnotic state, says, "I want more. I want more." Sabrina adds, "you want a younger man to fawn over you. Don't you. Somebody new." Jan says, "somebody new."

Out of nowhere, Sabrina brings her male assistant in. A younger man, not more than 28 years, who is taking courses in physical therapy from the local community college. He is interning at Sabrina's massage studio. The young man's name is Victor. Sabrina tells Victor, "massage on the front side." Victor says, "she is totally disrobed." Sabrina tells the man, "then, just massage the parts that aren't sexual." Victor starts rubbing Jan's legs. Sabrina whispers into Jan's ears, "remember what you were saying. Go ahead and say them louder." Jan recites, "I want more. I want more. Someone younger." Hearing the words, Victor looks puzzled. Jan continues reciting the mantra as Victor moves from the legs, avoiding the pelvis, and concentrates on the stomach. Rubbing the stomach does not seem to quiet Jan's from reciting the words over and over again. Sabrina interrupts Victor's hands and says, "she wants more. She is consenting." Sabrina takes Victor's hands and places it right on Jan's breasts and demands, "massage those." As the massage continues, Sabrina whispers, "he's here. Kiss him for all its worth." In a stupor-like state, Jan reaches up and pulls Victor's body down onto her kissing him uncontrollably. During this make out portion of the massage, Sabrina films it with a pocket-size video camera. Victor tries to remove the grasp of Jan and, when he succeeds, the camera instantly finds its way back into Sabrina's pocket. The damage is done.

Sabrina tells Victor, "thank you, Victor, she wants the strong hands of a man for some reason. You did a good job." Thinking to herself, if he reports the contact, the video will show him making out with an elderly person and he will never be licensed as a physical therapist or masseur. This will remain our secret.

When Victor leaves the room, Sabrina continues with the suggestions. "See, how that felt with a young man hovers over you in a sexual way. Like it was years before your marriage. It makes you feel so much younger than being with that old man. You are older but you still have the fire for true sexual satisfaction. If Glen isn't going to satisfy you, you need to find someone else. Repeat after me, 'If Glen isn't going to satisfy me, I need to find someone else.' Repeat it again." Jan repeats the latest suggestion, "if Glen isn't going to satisfy me, I need to find someone else."

The session is moving the way Sabrina had anticipated. "You need to leave Glen, remember his name is 'Money.' Take him for all his money. You are the Honey of 45 years for him. Honey needs Money. Repeat after me, "Honey needs Money. Honey needs Money. Get an attorney to get that Money. Attorney equals

Money. Attorney equals Money."

After 1 ½ hours, Jan comes out of the DTM and alcohol intoxication and has regain her senses but she has some difficulty walking straight. Before leaving, Sabrina offers a small cup, which she states is medicine, and Jan drinks it down. On the way out the door, Sabrina slaps Jan's behind, "you are so much better now. Remember, Honey needs Money." Jan recites it planting a kiss on Sabrina's cheek, "Honey needs Money. Attorney equals Money."

CHAPTER FORTY-TWO

Glen's Awakening

The die has been cast and Sabrina must act quickly to deliver the knockout punch. She calls Glen and privately whispers, "I had so much fun at the restaurant. Do you think we can do it again? I'll wear something slinky for you." Glen looks around to see that Jan is not nearby. "Why not. It's like a morgue around here. I don't know what's gotten into her, but she seldom says a word to me. She sees me and then says, 'money.'" She whispers to Glen, "she came in for a massage a day or so ago and kept saying, 'Honey needs Money.' She asked me to refer to her as 'Honey.' I'm not sure why. Come into my office so we can discuss this more privately today. Then, we can go to that restaurant you like." "Alright," says Glen, "I'll be over at 5 p.m."

Sabrina goes to her closet and picks out one of the sexiest cocktail dresses she owns with a slit up the back of the dress that goes to the bottom of her derriere. "This should be nitroglycerin in restarting his heart," says Sabrina laughing to herself. "The only angina he will experience is thinking about that trash woman back at home."

Glen comes into the studio and Sabrina, knowing the lay of the land, jumps into his muscular arms and he holds her without falling to either side. "I'm yours," she utters into his ear, nibbling it in the process. His reaction is not understated. He kisses her on the lips numerous times and slides his hand up her legs with delight. Seeing his level of interest rise, "I've got a big surprise for you tonight." He reacts and says, "I can't wait to see it." Sabrina corrects and says, "you mean feel it." Glen smiles.

Sabrina knows the next move. A move that will lay his cards on the table. "Do you know why I invited you to my office?" she asks. Glen replies, "no." "I have to tell you something in the strictest of confidence. Can you keep a secret?" she urges. Glen answers, "yes." Sabrina then takes Glen's right hand and passes it across her breasts and says, "cross my heart and hope to die." Glen smiles and says, "yes."

"She came in for a massage the other day and said to me, she wanted to be referred to as 'Honey.' I said, okay. I asked her why and she replied, 'I would like to make love to a younger man. I'm tired of that old dog.'" Glen almost interrupting says, "Jan said that?" Sabrina answers, "yes. And she said more." "What?" Glen requests. "She told me that she is only into you for the Money and asked me to refer to you as 'Money.' I told her, I can't do that. Glen is a paying customer. He has a name. Then, Jan says, 'we'll refer to Glen in code as 'Money.' I didn't know what to say. She kept saying over and over again, 'Honey needs Money.' And kept referring to you as Money, as independently wealthy. I tried to counter her by saying after 45 years of marriage, love is the important glue for the longevity of the relationship. She didn't buy it. She then went on to say you own apartment complexes. Is she lying?" asks Sabrina. Glen thinks for a moment, trusting in the conversation with Sabrina, "I own somewhere between 35 to 50 apartment complexes around the country." Making up the story as she goes, 'Jan says your net worth is around $70 million" (simply guessing at the amount). "No," he corrects the misstatement, "she is wrong I'm worth over $225 million," whispering as he articulates the amount. After hearing the amount, Sabrina almost faints and her legs give out causing her to fall to her knees. She thinks, to herself, "I've hit the mother lode of available sugar dads. Keep him interested." While on her knees, she places her head between his legs facing outward but not engaging in anything playful or sexual. While she is on her knees, he strokes her hair. They remain in that position for some time as if Sabrina is entranced herself in the prospect of marrying an elderly gentleman who is worth so much capital. She sees herself in a wedding gown ensconced in gold coins and bars flowing all around her head and body.

Glen is very saddened by what Sabrina has told him and has gone into a depressive funk. She thinks, "let's get it all out." She continues, "during the massage, she said that if she hires an attorney, she'll get your money, most of your money. She then started reciting over and over again, 'Attorney Equals Money; Attorney Equals Money.' She told me she wants to get most of your money and leave you with no assets."

Glen pushes back to a point of reality. "Look, she never said that before in our 45 years of marriage. It was only after we came to you for massages that she started saying these things. Maybe, you are the reason for all of this occurring. She never asked about my business; why would she care now."

Without the video, she would be on a cliff waiting for the final push. But with it, comes a ledge of truth. That is what she can land on. She says, "this too is very private. Can you keep it confidential?" Glen answers, "yes. I won't tell a soul." "Good," says Sabrina. "When she came in for the massage she requested the young man out front, my intern Victor, to massage her totally naked." Becoming more skeptical and seeing through Sabrina's efforts, he states, "I don't believe it or you. You are tricking me." Sabrina responds, "am I?" She pulls the video out and shows Victor massaging Jan's legs and then the stomach of the naked Jan. Through some computer generated imagery (CGI), Jan's hands grab Victor's hands and guides them to her breasts, hearing her say, "I want more. I want a younger man. Not an old dog." He sees her grab Victor's body and lowers it on to hers, where she starts kissing him madly.

Then, comes the *coup de grace* that converts Glen to Sabrina, when he hears Jan say: "if Glen isn't going to satisfy me, I need to find someone else." She repeats it several times.

Upon seeing the video, Glen says, "I'm done with her. After 45 years of marriage, we need to end this." "From what I've seen," says Sabrina, "I think you have every good reason to terminate it. You need to find happiness with someone who is not old and decrepit. She has apparently found happiness with a younger man. Let's go out to night and make it happen." She grabs his hand and places it in her hand. "We'll have so much fun at the restaurant."

CHAPTER FORTY-THREE

Public Transportation Avoided

It is commonly understood by citizens of the late-2050's that public transportation is a lesson in indoctrination. It started with subliminal messaging in advertising, then advanced into using algorithms to cater to the likes and dislikes of the consuming public, and then synthesized into commercial and political brainwashing. The temperament in the country was being controlled by so many outside influences that the government thought it would be beneficial to establish a "normalizing" control over the general public's perceptions of the world. It was like the use of fluoride in the water to better protect the public's dental needs or, similarly, the use of chlorine to eliminate bacteria from that very same water.

The government began to realize that the presence of so many pollutants in the public's streams of consciousness required a counterbalancing approach. If nothing was done, the minds and thoughts of others would be controlled by the internet and other sources of information. It began in the early 2010's and 2020's but grew to be harbingers of destructive misconduct and patterns that were upsetting religious, social, legal and political beliefs. Something had to be done to rein in these outside forces that were pulling people apart. If the counterbalancing measures were not implemented, anarchy would be the only down shot.

Regulations were implemented in legislative arenas and assemblies to permit a certain level of "impressionability" to avoid the use of the words "brainwashing," "propagandizing," "manipulating," or "programming." But, in essence, that was exactly what the regulations were meant to do. They were promulgated to protect the public's intellect on basic truths – one such truth was our freedoms must be tied to information that is real, factual and true. What good was freedom of press, freedom of speech, freedom of religion, if these outside forces could create a false narrative or preach falsehoods that would pollute the minds of its country people.

Those beliefs of influencing others' mindsets are in full array in the mid-2050's. It is a battle over the will to control people's perceptions and, understandably, it became the heart and soul of what people thought about in the basic individual, familial and large group setting. The suspicion was always -- what person is bringing in a thought or concept that would have a damaging impact upon an individual, a family, a group, or a government's halcyonic existence? Freedoms had to be protected from themselves at times. Freedom of religion could spawn a heresy or violation of a tenet of that faith by a twisted thought. Freedom of press could enable the promotion of a fiction that never occurred in the first place displacing truth and factual reporting.

The government saw no other option but to utilize "impressionability" as a response to these destructive, iconoclastic influences pervading at every level of our conscious lives. It determined that these influences would be first positioned in public arenas or assemblages where people congregate. Hence, it was implemented on public transportation. The concept worked well initially because people were "starving" for truth in every aspect of their lives. They got tired of being misled and influenced in ways that were destructive to society's goals and objectives. But, as time went on, people tired of those controls because, again, those outside sources were questioning why the government was engaging in its own "brainwashing" of the minds and outlooks of the public.

This caused people to avoid public transportation so they would not be susceptible to this new type of "brainwashing." There was no other road to go for the institutions to survive. If they sat back and did nothing, public opinion would be poisoned. If they tried to censor or block the outside influences, they might be tampering with those freedoms which the public enjoys. They had to participate in the "impressionability" or they would lose key segments of society. People traveling on public transportation got used to zoning out much of that information, but, in a way, they were glad that the government was doing something to promote the goodness and benefits of supporting individuality, family and other institutions.

CHAPTER FORTY-FOUR

Dr. Marjorie Birmbaum calls Director Russell Claybrook. "We've got a situation here. Can I be discreet?" says Marjorie. Knowing what discreet means from past experiences, Russell states, "You bet." "We have the report in on brain scans of Enbryo's genetic shaped subjects. The news is not good. Out of 962 subjects, there is 87.2% of the subject pool having smaller basal nuclei, anterior amygdaloid area (AAA) and cortical amygdala transition area (CATA) than the normal population of our control group." "What does that mean?" inquires Russell. "It means that lower volumes of amygdala nuclei, which involves fear modulation, stress responses, and social interaction may point to violent, aggressive behavior," Marjorie replies. "I still don't understand. I'm sorry, I'm not a scientist," concludes Russell.

Narrating the subject in more detail, Marjorie explains: "People who have serious psychological problems can be schizophrenic, sociopathic, or psychotic. Some have just general mental illness. As the report notes quoting from "<u>Associations between amygdala nuclei volumes, psychosis, psychopathy and violent offending</u>," published in *Psychiatry Research: Neuroimaging*, Vol. 319, January 2022, by Bell, Tesli, Gurholt, Rokicki, Hjell, Fischer-Vieler, Melle, Agartz, Andreassen, Rasmussen, Johansen, Friestad and Haukvik:

"Psychopathy is a multidimensional construct

characterized by a constellation of personality traits, such as grandiosity, impulsivity, lack of empathy and remorse (Fisher and Hany, 2019; Thomson et al. 2019) as well as manipulation of others, insincerity, lying, antisociality, and criminal offending (Wong and Oliver, 2015). Psychopathy is association with neuroanatomical abnormalities (Johanson et al., 2019), in specific brain circuits and areas, such as the amygdala and prefrontal cortex and the uncinate fasciculus which several regions of the limbic system, the cingulate, and the insular cortices, as well as of the hippocampi and the amygdalae (Johnson et al., 2019; Yang et al. 2010; Vieira et al. 2015). Psychopathic violence has been associated with deficient fear conditioning (Stahl, 2014) and poor fear reactivity (Thomson et al., 2019) which has been linked to attenuated amygdala reactivity (Birbaumer et al, 2005).

Our report confirms that study conducted on Associations Between Amygdala Nuclei Volumes, Psychosis, Psychopathy and Violent Offending establishes a correlation that "volume reduction, and supposedly dysfunction, in the basal nucleus, which is involved in emotion, cognition, and modulation of stress, make aggressive behavior more likely." (Bell et al., 2022).

What this all means, is that the majority, if not, most of Enbryo's subjects have volume reductions in the basal nucleus, AAA and CATA areas. Thus, they have more of a propensity to commit violent criminal acts."

"This is terrible news," as he stumbles on the words. He adds, "what can we do?" Marjorie shaking her head says, "there are some alternatives but they have not developed with any promising results. One thing is certain the smaller amygdala volumes means we have greater depressive symptom severity with the Enbryo population. The smaller the amygdala volume the less connectivity to other parts of the brain and the less inhibitory controls in place, meaning more anti-social, violent behavior." He responds, "we may be through if this report gets out. What should we do?" he asks. "We need to bury it in the Mariana Trench so no one can find it. We are not obligated to report this and we can hide it until a mechanism is developed to alter the size and volume of the nuclei in the basal amygdala, AAA and CATA," whispers Marjorie.

One intern called Rudy Escobedo happened upon the opened report on Marjorie's desk when Marjorie stepped out for coffee earlier that day before the call with Russell. He took some pictures of the report quickly while she was away. He actually was a participant in the study having himself been genetically shaped and was extremely curious as to why Enbryo was conducting the survey in the first place and, secondly, what were the results of the survey. He had figured that requesting the pool of genetically shaped subjects to submit to a brain scan may have been an internal alarm signaled by the company that something was terribly wrong. The curiosity was eating him alive. When he saw the results it all made sense to him. When he got mad at something, he ignited a conflagration of temper and anger that was not easily manageable. He was only 18 years old and found himself throughout his life battling people for very slight transgressions or "peccadilloes" as he called them. One time he punched an older gentleman for calling him "too tall to take down." That he thought in retrospect was not a peccadillo just a way to get out of a tussle with a young boy. His reaction was uncontrollable. He punched him in the face three to four times causing some bruises and cuts to the face. Though Rudy never apologized later for the skirmish neither did the older gentleman. He felt like maybe he had provoked the fight by saying some baneful words to the youth. He never filed a report with the police nor sought prosecution for the pummeling.

By the time Marjorie returned to her office, Rudy was back at his desk. She looked at him closely to see if he had entered her room but, with that passing glance, Rudy did not shed a glimpse of guilt or betrayal on his face. He was angry but in a different way. He was crowned by his peers as a strikingly good-looking boy with genius tendencies for brilliance. That was not the cause of his anger. His anger was rooted in what now has become a dysfunctional brain that could engage in violently abusive behavior. He did not know when it would be spurred into action. But it was a matter of serious concern to him. He knew there would be a time and place that the report would be revealed to his brothers and sisters of the newly-developing technology.

CHAPTER FORTY-FIVE

Judicial Roadblock Reopened

Several months after the report was "buried," a defense attorney for Tyesha contacts Marjorie Birmbaum. "Hi, I'm Lance Essex with the Public Defenders' Office and I'm inquiring into a connection between Tyesha Biggerstaff and the Dirk Rainjoy's criminal matters. Have you heard of either or both these cases?" Marjorie answers, "yes," in a very subdued voice. "Has Enbryo conducted any studies or case histories on these two or others that have been genetically shaped?" states Lance. Very suspicious, she asks, "Is it just you and me on the phone here?" "Yes," Lance replies. "I don't believe we have done any studies or surveys on Tyesha or Dirk directly as a result of the criminal cases. And we have not been asked to do any studies." Lance does not give up at that point and asks a follow-on question: "Have you conducted any personal studies into the brains of genetically-shaped individuals?" he asks. "Have I?" she inquires. Then adds, "No. I haven't." "Do you know if your firm has conducted any such studies or surveys," he asks. "Not that I am aware of. I get so many reports on my desks, I can't recall seeing such a survey or study on genetically-shaped subjects." Playing the company line, Marjorie adds, "we just get parents and subjects reaching out to us thanking us for making their lives so much better. There does not seem to be any criticism or discontent. Hopefully, that answers your questions." Lance realizing that Marjorie is being short with him says, "Yes. That answers my questions. Thank you for your time."

The trial in the Tyesha Biggerstaff case proceeded with jury selection and the presentation of the prosecution's case that could only be described as "indestructible." They had the testimony of Prosperity that showed how she was programmed by Tyesha to commit an attempted murder. Fortunately, Prosperity, given her loyal employment history at McElroy and the brainwashing she suffered at the hands of Tyesha, was provided prosecutorial immunity to testify against Tyesha. Tyesha's criminal intent was spilt blood all over that program that was spun to mind-control Prosperity to kill. Thus, the *Mens Rea* for the act could be easily achieved through the software program.

The Brainwasher's Defense was ill-conceived and ludicrous to present to a very interested jury. The nationwide spectacle enamored both the jury and the audience to their own entrancement to the case. Once the defense flopped, the jury returned a verdict to murder in the first degree within the short span of 1 hour and 14 minutes.

Stoked by the ravenous appetite of the public's interest in the case, a neurosurgeon at Harvard Medical School, Dr. Harold Steinwald, picked up the gauntlet to explore the issue of genetic shaping. The University was also a little concerned how someone so gifted and educated at the finest universities could succumb to such a deplorable act. Harold contacted Tyesha at the prison she was assigned and asked her to do a brain scan to query whether gene shaping may have been the culprit in her behavior. Tyesha, at first hesitant about submitting to such a scan, finally, consented to the procedure at the behest of her counsel because it may provide new evidence for a new trial.

The scan took place on August 15th and, shortly thereafter, Harold was reviewing the scans with a team of medical doctors at Harvard. The doctors reached a consensus that the basal nucleus, anterior amygdaloid area and cortical amygdala transition area had a smaller size and volume than the normal human brain. Their conclusion based upon the analysis and earlier reports and studies is that Tyesha had a greater propensity to commit psychotic violent acts.

Once the results surfaced, Lance Essex stepped on the accelerator and asked for a new trial. Because Lance had attempted to get that evidence from Enbryo and it was not available, the trial judge felt that an earnest effort was made by Tyesha and her legal team to avail herself of some other defense than the Brainwasher's Defense. He granted a new trial based upon the organic aspects of the new research and recent studies. The amygdala size and volume could have meddled with the level of a man-endangering state of mind so that the jury could have found for a lesser included offense than murder one.

With that successful result, Dirk Rainjoy was cogently asked by his counsel to undergo a brain scan that may shorten his stint in prison. Dr. Steinwald agreed to conduct and analyze the results of the brain scan.

The two cases sparked curiosity at all levels of the scientific and medical communities.

CHAPTER FORTY-SIX

Damage Control

Enbryo's Board of Directors has asked the executive officers to attend a corporate meeting along with Dr. Marjorie Birmbaum to discuss the recent developments posited by Harvard Medical Hospital. Russell Claybrook reported to the Board that a study had been conducted on 962 genetically-shaped subjects of Enbryo who had been brain-scanned. The study was performed approximately 1 year ago and the results showed that "87.2% of the subject pool had smaller basal nuclei, anterior amygdaloid area (AAA) and cortical amygdala transition area (CATA) than the normal population of our control group." The 7 other Directors and one Chairman expressed shock over the results asking Claybrook why these results were not posted earlier with the Board. Claybrook answers, "we could not confirm that high percentage would be conducive to engaging in criminal behavior. We simply looked at brain parts and examined size and volume. We did not conduct any studies on the 962 to ascertain their proclivity to criminality or violent behavior. Chairman Soderbaugh interjects during Claybrook's explanation and says, "why was that not done? There were studies conducted in the last 20-30 years that delved into the association of size and volume of brain parts and the commission of criminal acts." Claybrook answers, "we made a judgment call that it would not be in the best interest of Enbryo to conduct that test for obvious reasons." Chairman Soderbaugh unleashes his fury at that remark, saying: "you thought to play God and bury this report in some obscure way to protect the best interests of Enbyro. We are on the verge of major litigation if the Harvard Medical studies hold water. We cannot cover this up. We must cooperate or we will be criminally prosecuted out of existence." Corporate Counsel for Enbyro suggests, "let's send out a news release that genetically shaping does in fact result in smaller limbic system volume and size but there is no confirmed proof on the part of Enbryo that this leads to criminal behavior or violent abusive acts." Chairman Soderbaugh reacts saying, "that's a better strategy than just hiding our research. Then, if investigators want to examine the report they will find that we were true blue relative to the quantifiable number of those brain-scanned and the results." Corporate Counsel adds, "if those investigators ask why we did not take it a step further to evaluate the criminal histories of the brain-scanned subjects, we can argue the right of privacy, medical privilege, HIPAA and other protections. Further, we did not feel that as a genetic-shaping company we should be wading into private criminal information." "Yes," says Soderbaugh, "we can stratify our level of protection through privilege in order to justify why we did not conduct a phase two study into psychotic violent behavior. Make sure those reports are cleansed of anything that might refer to those other studies on psychotic violent behavior. By redaction and re-writing the report, we should be able to avoid a major hit on litigation and save our jobs. To do nothing will bring down the house." The Board meeting adjourns on that note.

CHAPTER FORTY-SEVEN

First Day On The Job

Samantha Redding, a young 18-year old, was so excited about the prospects of working for a 7-year old boy who lives in a mansion nestled on a hill in Beverly Hills. She had heard that the boy's father had been institutionalized for mental illness after a fire broke out at the home. It took a year or so for the home to be rebuilt but it is more elegant than before. Having come from a same town near Duluth, Minnesota, called Hibbing, she was filled with wild tales of Hollywood and the local celebrity, Robert Zimmerman aka Bob Dylan. She thoroughly read up on him and listened to his music. Though not an absolute devotee of his music, she sparkled when she thinks of the mountain of fame and fortune he realized from his talents. She desperately wanted to succeed. So, she came to Southern California like so many other beauties, panning for gold on the rivers of influence, power and excess. She got this assignment from a nanny service out of Encino. When she got the news of the opportunity and that she had been selected, she began to think that angels were swirling around her guiding her down those very rivers. As a young girl, impressionable and coy, she possessed a very fanciful imagination, disconnected from reality but believed that fate was by her side.

She envisioned that she would swoon this boy off the face of the earth, though there is now an 11-year difference in age. She knew about sex and had engaged in it a couple of times but was not too smitten with it. As her female prerogative, she knew how to enlist that sexuality in ways that would captivate her prey. Her mission was to enrapt the boy into her spell and then control him in every way, possibly, culminating in his marrying her or signing legal papers to transfer properties and stocks to her. As one can see, her naivete had its limitations. No plan had been executed as to how this would all succeed; it was kind of a blunderbuss approach. That was expected given her age and lack of skill sets in this art of persuasion.

The one thing paramount in her constitution unbeknownst to her is the absence of gene shaping; her parents not having the financial clout to afford such privilege. She is attractive with reddish hair, taller than the average fair-skinned girl, and not blessed with proportions that would emphasize her figure. She was flat all the way around. One of her chummy girlfriends back home commented in a joking manner on one occasion that she was "Miss Flatirons;" a name she despised. Samantha pushed the girl in her right shoulder quite abruptly causing the friend to immediately repent and recant what she had just spoken. Samantha knew when she came to SoCal that the only way she could compete in this formidable market was to fly with the eagles and not trot with the turkeys. On arrival here, she saw opportunities but she also saw who got those opportunities. She had to look her best and the best required contouring her body to make it most appealing to both the female and male eye, with emphasis upon the former.

There was one troubling aspect about the assignment. The agency informed her that the former nanny had shown peculiarities in her behavior, leading up to serious mental illness; hence, the reason for bringing in a new nanny. What caused a lot of concern was Samantha, as part of her job duties, was to medicate the nanny periodically throughout the day, making sure that she took the prescribed medications at the times and intervals required. She never inquired as to the reasons for the mental illness when her imagination got the best of her in fantasizing she would be solely in charge of the boy and that the former nanny was ill-equipped to handle any domestic matters.

For her first day, she wanted to look her best. She primped and preened herself to look like a natural beauty, wearing a cute laced blouse with a multi-colored skirt with wavy reds, blues and whites. She pulled her hair back and rolled it into small bun that rested on the nape of her neck.

She arrives at the mansion and is completely overwhelmed by its size and stately qualities. Taking a small frontal tour of the home she smiles and says, "if I play my cards right, this could be my home forever," swirling around in a circle of glee. She comes out of the illusion and refocuses on the job at hand. "I need to treat this job with sincerity and," searching for the right word, finishes by saying, "passion. That's right, passion. The more passionate I am about the job, the better my chances are at winning his heart."

She enters the front porch and strokes her hair back one last time and presses the entry button. Minutes pass and she presses again. No answer. She gazes through the windows, which are slightly tinted, but can't see much. She returns to the front door and again presses the entry button. No answer again. Suddenly, the door clicks unlocked and then slowly opens. No one is there to greet her but she assumes she is free to enter. Walking through the atrium, she views the magnificent sculptures and paintings positioned throughout the entryway, atrium and front of the mansion. Curious as to why no one is around she continues searching for the presence of the boy or someone to receive her. Happening through the library, she is totally in bliss upon seeing the cherry wood beams and walls of the library. Looking around and seeing no one, she recreates the dancing swirl she did outside, imagining she is an actress on a stage; she is anyway.

Then, she stops and hears a slight pulsating sound of a Latin salsa beat get louder and louder. It fills the room. She looks up and sees Algar staring at her from the second floor of the library. She is frozen unsure what her next step is. For the longest time the music plays, she stares at him and he at her. The words descend from the upper floor like a demand from a demigod or the Creator himself, "dance, dance." She is paralyzed like she has been turned into a pillar of salt like Lot's wife. Algar orders her again, "dance, dance, dance." Samantha thinks, "what is he doing? Does he really want me to dance?" Looking at the library again, she says to herself, "remember be passionate. This is your opportunity to impress." She starts to move her legs slowly in a dance. With a bundle of nerves, she is out of cadence with the syncopation of the beat, causing Algar to comment, "faster, faster, faster."

The music gets louder to the point it is beginning to hurt Samantha's ears, she tries covering them up but she has to dance faster to keep up with the beat. The beat speeds up more and more. Samantha finally falls to the ground in exhaustion but stands up again, looking up at Algar. "Keep dancing. Don't stop," Algar edicts, as he disappears around a corner and stays out of sight. Samantha keeps dancing looking around for the boy to return or greet her. An hour passes, the music is still playing, and Samantha sits on the floor exhausted.

Algar enters the room and says, "stand up and follow me." Samantha gets up, extending her hand but he turns before any salutation could be engaged. He hands Samantha pills that are to be given to Rebecca every 4 hours.. Samantha reads the labels on the prescribed medication and says to Algar, just to engage in some communication, "this is an anti-depressant, right?" Algar does not respond but continues to walk up the stairs to Rebecca's room. Reaching her room, "give her one pill every 4 hours. Go," says Algar and opening the door to her room. Algar does not enter but walks away.

Rebecca's room is dark and dungeon-like. Samantha can see a figure in the bed but it is too nondescript given the lack of light to ascertain the features. She walks some distance in the large bedroom and opens a floor to ceiling curtain that sprays the light throughout the room. She walks over to the bed and sees Rebecca sleeping soundly face up. Samantha looks at Rebecca in shock saying privately, "what the hell happened to her. She looks terrible. Her hair is completely shaved off and there is a definite bruising and redness at her temples. Why is she wearing a Halloween costume dressed as Little Red Riding Hood? She is a grown woman." She thinks a little more on the subject, "am I a nanny for this lunatic or for the little dictator," hesitating, "or both?" She opens the container thinking, "he ordered me to give her a pill, so that's what I'll do." She takes one pill out and opens Rebecca's mouth and places the pill inside her mouth. She thinks, "shouldn't she drink this with water?" She looks at the label and there is no mention of taking the medication with fluids. She then thinks, "maybe it absorbs on the tongue and doesn't need fluid to wash it down. I don't know. She seems like she is sleeping through all of this so if I gave her a drink while she is unconscious, she will definitely choke on it." She concludes, "I'm just leaving it on her tongue." She looks at Rebecca and thinks, "this girl is in bad shape. How could this happen in such a nice home as this?" She notices that this Red Riding Hood is wearing handcuffs. "Why is she wearing handcuffs? Little Red Riding Hood was never handcuffed? But, then she puts the whole scenario of events into focus and states, "she's on a suicide watch and I'm her watcher." Nevertheless, this is a question she will bring up to Algar as soon as she reconnects with him. She leaves the room.

As she walks downstairs, her list of questions grows in number. When she gets to the bottom of the stairs, Algar is present holding a costume of wonder woman and says, "wear." Samantha looks at the outfit and thinks, "this is so strange, but it is a child of tender years who worships heroes and heroines. If it were a grown man that had asked me to wear it, I'd be out the door in a second." Stalling for time, he hands the costume to Samantha and she looks at it closely and then looks at Algar. Sensing this may be the moment for an introduction, she announces, "Hi, I'm Samantha and you are…?" No reply. Algar says, "wear." Ignoring the salutation, Samantha is somewhat miffed about the lack of his social grace and says, "Thank you. But I have my own clothes. I don't need to wear this." She attempts to hand the costume back, but Algar pushes it back at her and says, "wear. Wear," in a louder voice. Samantha is at the crossroads of the opportunity. She either puts it on or walks out the door. She thinks, "I really don't have an option. This is a perfect opportunity to make it here in LA and be part of the social aristocracy. That woman upstairs was wearing a costume, so the boy must have a hard on for cosplay. I can live with that. It's just a costume; I'm not surrendering my soul or anything. If I walk out of this stately mansion, I may be surrendering to a life filled with poverty and hard work. If I play my cards right, I could own this house." Hesitating no longer, "I'll wear the costume." Little did Samantha know, she had conceded some control to the boy, but she figured in the long run she would win it all back.

CHAPTER FORTY-EIGHT

The Nanny's Nanny

The atmosphere in two rooms so close together could not be so different. Samantha awakes to a sunny day with it beaming through the windows of her room. She looks up at the ornate ceiling with wood sculpted angels leading to fancy crown molding. The satin sheets of her bed caress her youthful body as she stretches and massages her legs and arms with the contact. She smiles at the good luck she has found at that palatial extravaganza of a home. Reflecting back on the previous day, "I didn't sacrifice my image by dancing and wearing the costume. He's just a boy and needs to fantasize. Without a mom or dad, he may be lost in a world of cosplay to avoid the reality of the situation. I can use the character of wonder woman to gain access to his soul and push my slinky body into his face to take charge over his life, his home and his wealth." She repeats again, saying, "I like that – his LIfE, his hoME and his WEALTH," creating a useful slogan, "Lie Me N Wealth." She laughs after reciting the slogan a second time.

Curious about the girl next door, Samantha goes to social media and studies the images of Rebecca. Looking at pictures of her in wet clothes over time was disturbing, but not as disturbing as seeing her with a shaved head, wearing prison clothes and then viewing the video of herself smacking her butt with a stick. "She's one sick woman. Hold it! She's wearing handcuffs. Maybe, she's a criminal and not on suicide watch. I need to be careful.

She could be dangerous." She dwells more on her immediate comforts and squirms a little in the bed, feeling a sense of happiness and good fortune. She stops for a moment thinking, "what if the nanny gets healthy again? What happens if she resumes her job over this household and Algar? I'll be out on the streets and crawling back to Hibbing as a prodigal daughter. I better do my job and win this young dude over before she comes back to health. He'll boot her to the door and I'll be the princess of the manor."

Just then, her eyes float over to the costume she had initially identified as a Wonder Women outfit she had worn the day before. But something was different about it. This outfit did not have a red top, blue and white star shorts, gold waist belt, and red boots. It looks strangely in black. Samantha looks at it for the longest time, without getting up, wondering if the way the light shines through the room would darken the red and blue colors of the outfit. Curiosity gets the better of her and she rises from the bed and scurries over to the outfit. There are no reds and blues. What she thinks are stars are actually scorpions ready to attack. Disbelieving her own eyesight, she takes the hangered outfit over to the direct sunlight and sees that the outfit is in black with only some white background here and there. She thinks, "I distinctly remember it was red and blue. Now, it's black. Did he change my outfit? How'd he do that?" She rushes into the bathroom and sees a small note next to black makeup and lipstick. "Put on with your 'Under Woman' outfit." She looks at the makeup and lipstick and states out loud: "This is going too far. I can't wear this. This is so gloomy and depressing. I'm going to take this down to him and shove it in his face." A little despair creeps in causing her to envision the prospects of not having the job there. She then rationalizes, "he can't be that bad. I can twist him around my little finger. I'm in charge here. I'm the nanny, I'm the adult and he's the child. I'll play this game." She dresses in the Under Woman outfit and applies the black make-up as eye shadow, black eye-liner, slight blackish blush, and black lipstick.

She looks at herself and smiles, "When you catch a glimpse of me, Sweetie, you will want me around all the time instead of that nutcase nanny," wiggling her rear in the mirror.

The climate in the adjacent room could not be more contrasting. The darkness fuses with a sense of regret and sorrow. Rebecca wakes to tears streaming down her face. The regimen of pills she has received has taken her far away from a nutritious diet and it is starting to show all over her skinny body. It gives the appearance that she is emaciated. She raises her head from the pillow having been in bed for three days almost unmoving. She is disoriented and dizzy. She falls back on to the pillow. She feels a tightness around her upper thighs on both sides; something constricting the blood flow. Reaching down to that section, the sound of handcuffs clang together. She shakes her head at the thought of the stupid debacle she is in.

She slowly sits up and then turns her legs to the bedside. That simple exercise has left her tired and huffing a little. Rising to her feet, she staggers over to a full-length standing mirror and looks at herself, mesmerized by what she sees. "What has happened to me? I used to be so attractive. My face has been jolted by electric current and my head shaved many times, including at the hospital. I'm being prosecuted as a criminal, and I'm in protective custody of a young ogre who dominates every aspect of my life." She looks at the silly Red Riding Hood costume and sees her hands manacled and she shouts out loud, "I'm not your puppet anymore." She rips off the costume with some difficulty, exposing her breasts. She now spies the reason for her upper leg discomfort – little girl panties with circus animals displayed in various colors. "What is that doing on me? I don't remember putting those on." She looks around the room and in the two closets and cannot find another garment or underclothing. Mad at the prospects of no other clothing, she exclaims: "If that's the way you want it, I'm not wearing your fuckin' costumes anymore." The little girl panties cover very little of Rebecca's pubic area and seeing that, "I don't care anymore. There is nothing I am ashamed of."

She takes another long look in the mirror in silence and then sees a vision of herself hanging from a tree. She turns away from looking at the mirror somewhat out of fright but entranced by what she has just seen. She returns her gaze to the mirror. She sees herself waving to come closer to the mirror. As if under the spell of the mirror, she comes closer and closer to the mirror and, then, as if it is from her point of view, the figure in the mirror places the noose around the viewing Rebecca and Rebecca goes through a choking sensation that drops her to the floor. There is no rope around her neck but she reacts as if it is. She yells out, "help me, help me. I'm being hanged."

Hearing the sounds coming from Rebecca's room, Samantha leaves her room to see what is happening. She passes by a table containing the medications that Rebecca is to receive. "I better take one just in case," taking a pill out of the container, then heading for Rebecca's room.

Samantha opens the locked room from the outside and hurries in to see Rebecca still gagging on the floor. She rushes down to her. Immediately, Rebecca's eyes fall upon Samantha and the gagging stops. She studies her face closely and says, "Who are you?" "I'm Samantha. I'm your nanny, I mean, your caretaker." Rebecca sees that Samantha has a pill in her hand and hears her say, "I have to give you this," referring to the pill. Rebecca pushes Samantha off of her, saying, "bitch, I don't need you," and scampers out the opened door.

By the time Samantha gets to the opened door, Rebecca is nowhere to be seen. She slowly goes downstairs and makes her way to the kitchen. She enters the kitchen and there, in a corner of the room, is Rebecca holding a knife saying, "don't come near. I will kill you. You hear me." Samantha trying to remain calm holds out the pill saying, "this is good for you. It will make you relax." Rebecca responds, "stay away from me Miss Bitch or I'll stab you." Samantha continues advancing toward Rebecca and she slashes out at Samantha coming close to cutting her. She side steps Samantha and hastens out the door and up the steps to her bedroom.

Samantha follows behind trying to keep up with Rebecca's stride and speed. She trips going up the stairs. When she enters Rebecca's room, she sees Rebecca standing in the casement of a window that is flung open with a cord from a lamp attached around her neck, her arms held up and out and legs fully apart facing the outside garden.

Samantha goes silent at the sight and slowly enters. In a loud voice, Rebecca shrieks out, "Redeem me from misfortune. Forgive all my sins." Not sure what Rebecca is plotting to do, Samantha leaps at Rebecca's lower legs engaging what appears to be a tackle but sets off in motion Rebecca's falling out of the window into a sycamore tree where the lamp gets caught on one of its gigantic branches resulting in Rebecca hanging from the tree. As she swings back and forth, she looks at Samantha's face and smiles. Slowly, Rebecca dies of strangulation. Samantha is overcome from the hanging and covers her face with her hands at the sight. Samantha lets out a burst of emotion and screams as loud as she can.

A little while later, Algar enters Rebecca's room and says to Samantha, "you pushed her out the window." Samantha says, "no, I didn't." The video shows otherwise. The fact that Rebecca is found in just panties and the video shows Samantha wearing a dark bizarre outfit at the time of Rebecca's death does not bode well for her. Algar shows the video to Samantha and, with some adjustments made by Algar, Samantha pushes Rebecca out the window. When the matter is finally reported, the police investigate and determine it was suicide, especially with the cord around the neck of the victim. However, Algar says to Samantha, "I'll give the police the video, if you don't follow my orders." The boy now is in charge of Samantha.

CHAPTER FORTY-NINE

It started out in a small newspaper in San Jose, California, and, within a day, it exploded into major nationwide news with every news agency, outlet, and enterprise carrying the story of how genetic shaping causes the reduction in size and volume of certain parts of the brain leading to high incidence of criminal behavior. World news picked up the story and headlines were running: "Beauty is in the Eyes of the Killer," "Beauty is power; watch for its sword," "Beauty, Brains and Booty Can Kill," "When you look good, you feel evil," "Where Beauty Begins, Life Ends," and "Don't turn your back on Beauty."

The stories included the Rainjoy and Biggerstaff prosecution and updates on how they were proceeding with new trials and appeals.

The results of these articles were general suspicions that genetic shaped brains were a liability to be around. Most genetically shaped brains were in the bodies of people under the age of 30 so they were easier to identify.

Societal reaction was fear that association with a beautiful young person could be dangerous to one's health. Given the infusion of outside sources arising from the internet and social media, beautiful young people are being "criminalized." Some sources related that genetically shaped young people were like firearms ready to go off at a moment's notice. It was desirable to hang around an older person who had natural or, even, artificial beauty, but to gravitate towards a genetically-shaped person (GSP) is hazardous to your life. Like smoking unfiltered cigarettes, "it is just a matter of time before it chokes you to death."

As the truth faded from the stories, the incipience of falsehoods slowly crept into the discussion, feeding a frenzy that those not genetically-shaped should cut off any association with GSP's.

GSP's filed lawsuits against everybody and everything for discrimination in privileges and accommodations, and they certainly filed against Enbryo for the ostracism from society and other positions of distinction. Some employers refused to hire GSP's claiming that the laws required a safe, healthy and wholesome work environment and that hiring a GSP could violate those laws. Just the threat that a Doberman Pinscher could become unglued and engage in violent psychotic behavior was reason enough not to hire a GSP. GSP's sued employers who found a way to terminate them for various reasons claiming discrimination and retaliation, but there were no laws in place that protected GSP's, plus GSP's were never regarded, historically, as being victims of invidious discrimination. When GSP's turned their attention to suing prospective employers for refusal to hire, the employers generally mounted a "loaded gun" defense, saying the gun had been cocked and was ready to fire. Most of the time the defense prevailed in front of a judge or jury. Only, in rare circumstances, when the GSP did not have a history of violent behavior, probably, falling within the 12% to 13% who never developed any psychotic violent behavior, did he or she prevail against the prospective employer.

In political and religious circles, GSP's were being barred from advancement. Relative to priests, before they could be ordained, background checks were conducted by the Church to guarantee that they were not genetically-shaped. If they were, they were nullified from continuing with their education. If they ran for political office, just the idea the candidate was gene-shaped was enough for voters to cast their vote for the other candidate.

There were no party loyalties in this area. A democrat would vote for a non-GSP republican and vice versa.

GSP's did not wear their badge of dishonor well. Once they were labeled "outcasts" at every level of society, business and government, they did not withdraw into their shells never to return to the light of day. Some banded together and began plotting against the institutions that excluded them. Having well-greased minds, these GSP's developed clever ways to bring down those institutions, attempting methods that were used by the Unabomber of yesteryear. Bombs, explosives, incendiaries, anthrax, thallium, and other creative ways to kill one or more people.

When bombs went off at government buildings and churches and synagogues, the non-gene-shaped began to band together against these sinister forces.

Having had a good two decades to develop genetically-shaped people, it could be said that there was a small minority of the country that fell into that category. In other words, there was a lot of people out there that fit the definition of GSP. The public's perception was that the "country was coming unglued" and those principles that have long governed our country are now under assault from a large body of people who have been programmed to kill." Some of the public started a chant, "the Bigger the Staff, the Bigger the Shaft," referring to Biggerstaff and her ability to program people to kill.

The publicity surrounding the GSP's turned the international world into an endemic of paranoia. Many people disassociated with any young beautiful person. The unfortunate prospect with all this is that there were naturally beautiful people who were not genetically altered in some way. They felt discriminated too. Many of them carried birth certificates with them to prove that they were not genetically shaped but that was not enough to allay the fears that people had. The outside sources had ramped up the hysteria by claiming that GSP's were attempting to pass themselves off as not genetically-shaped. People did not know who to trust or who to distrust. The better plan of action is to discontinue any involvement with beautiful people altogether.

One advertising company thought itself cute by treating a beautiful person as a virus attacking the bodies of less attractive people. That advertising campaign worked well in sowing the seeds of malcontent and further labeling GSP's as misfits. Some saw beautiful people as a threat to the very existence of society. When they saw a beautiful person walking down the street, they would scoff at the person saying, "stay away from me," or simply walk another way. Others were outright rude and were heard to comment, "you have no place in our world. Leave." The scorn heaped upon beautiful people had such a resounding effect that some beautiful people had plastic surgery performed to change their facial features to homely: large noses, jutting jaws, thin lips, sunken faces, and high foreheads. Anything they could do to make themselves appear average looking. Plastic surgeons had to change their directions from beautifying to disfiguring to obtain an average look. They made money either way. Women would come in requesting, "make my face unattractive," "I don't mind jowls," "can you enlarge and widen my nose." Some went so far as to go to their cosmetic dentist and have him stain or create imperfections in their teeth to reduce their appeal of their smile. One young attractive man, who could not afford plastic surgery, took a sharp razor blade to his face and hacked away at it with various strokes to create a "scarface."

The age of beautiful people seemed to be coming to an end. Younger people were stricken with a social disease: first, by just being young; and, second, being attractive. It created a social stigmata that many young people could not bear or wear.

There was no way to quell the interest in the story. It had countermanded everything since the beginning of humankind.

People, at all ages, including infants, are drawn to and captivated by pretty, beautiful people. They are a magnet for our eyes and desires. Then, something happens, and now they are a hindrance and peril to our lives; they must be avoided at every turn.

Law enforcement was not blind to the social changes and mores of the day. It was no longer racial profiling but GSP profiling. If someone was stopped for a traffic offense and he or she was beautiful, he or she would be asked to exit the vehicle for a further pat down. If they were young and beautiful, they could be expected to be detained for a lot longer than those that did not fit that demographic.

When it came to the courts, a once sympathetic judge or jury in giving a beautiful person a lighter sentence changed with that person receiving stiffer fines, longer sentences and severe punishment. The Texas legislature passed a law that if you are GSP and commit a violent crime, a first strike warrants life imprisonment.

Despite the tremendous ridicule and denigration to GSP's, they were still entitled to live their lives and could not be exiled away to a deserted island somewhere in the Indian Ocean. Some empathetic groups sought ways for their treatment and some brain surgeries were enlisted to enlarge the volume or shape of the limbic system. But, given the sheer numbers of those GSP's, solutions were not easy to come by.

GSP's went underground, when all else failed, trying to limit their exposure to public places, gatherings and stay away from the public's view. It was better to go into hiding than to feel the wrath of people straight on.

CHAPTER FIFTY

Repentance

Far from the newsprint reeling off of machines at a furious pace, in the darkness only lit by moonlight, Gizpaco glides down the river of sorrow sculling for any poor soul that may be alive or dead. It is as if it is his ritual to guide those lost or abandoned souls to a place of serenity. Gizpaco has felt his whole life that his purpose is to guide people in the right direction for salvation. His gondola cuts the water so quietly this night that not even the dace reacts to its disturbance. That back and forth stroking of his oar creates a continuous forward motion in the water. He looks around from bank to bank for the presence of a target. The target has been requested by Dia. She put the order in for an esophagus, stomach and large intestines. As the years have gone by, he has gotten better equipped at the delivery of body parts to her and carries a scalpel that she has provided him with to complete his task.

As he glances at each bank, he thinks, "the warm sky meets the warm water and the moon has spilled its light all over it." He enjoys being out on this river tonight and trawls it with keen eyes that recede into a sunken face. A mosquito buzzes his ear and he swipes at it. They are a common pest that invade his thoughts this summer night.

Making his way down the river, he sees a lantern burning alongside the right bank and he focuses on it like a moth swirling around candlelight. He sees a lone stranger sitting upslope wearing waterproof fishing pants and boots. He has a fishing line extended from its pole to the water. Seeing the gondola, fisherman mutters something in Russian that Gizpaco cannot neither understand or hear.

Not to disturb where the line enters the water, Gizpaco navigates his boat to a place short of the entry point and steps onto the right bank. The lantern provides some light for this lone man to see a tall, lanky bent over man with an old black farmer's hat approach him. The man grabs his fishing knife and holds it by his side out of sight of Gizpaco. Getting closer he sees that Gizpaco is carrying an axe.

The man backs up just a little in a defensive posture. Gizpaco says, "may I sit?" Somewhat hesitant and somewhat relieved that Gizpaco is not wielding the operative end of the axe, the man says, "Have a seat."

The conversation is limited with both men staring at the lantern some distance off, in the uncomfortable position of not knowing what to say. Breaking the ice, the man says, "what brings you out to these parts?" Gizpaco nods over to his gondola and says no more. "Nice boat," says the lone man. "Your name?" asks Gizpaco. "Grigori," says the man. Gizpaco quips back, "Russian?" To which Grigori answers, "yes." Grigori asks, "fishing?" Gizpaco thinks and then answers, "in a way."

Both men run out a words and look at the water flowing by. After some time sitting there, Gizpaco asks, "Catch anything?" Grigori answers, "just a cold." Showing no reaction to the remark, Gizpaco adds, "you must repent if you want to save yourself." Grigori says in broken English, "Done nothing to repent." Gizpaco looks into the face of Grigori and says, "you have." Grigori states, "you don't know." "I see blood all over your hands," announces Gizpaco. Grigori raises his hands and chuckling says, "I'm clean." Gizpaco responds, "no, you kill," and with that raises his axe quickly and severs Grigori's left hand from his forearm. Screaming in agony, Grigori holds his left forearm, gets up and runs up slope with Gizpaco chasing behind him.   But Gizpaco's hunched-over posture makes him little match for the fast running Grigori, who makes it to his car. The last words he hears from Gizpaco is "repent for your sins. Repent before you die."

To prevent excessive bleeding, Grigori ties a small rope he found in his car around his forearm to prevent from bleeding to death. He rushes to an emergency medical facility. He refuses to discuss how he lost his hand despite repeated efforts of the ER nurse and doctor to obtain that information. He did not return to find his severed hand thinking that, whatever that creature was, he did not want to meet again in his life. That creature took more than his left hand. He reached into his soul and changed his life forever.

After the bleeding had been properly treated and with "repent for you sins; repent before you die," echoing in his head, he went to the police station and reported his involvement in Wade Terriff and Monte Enright's disappearance. He fingered his partner, Peter, and identified Seve Aguado as the perpetrators of the murders. He would take whatever punishment was meted out but felt that his role was more of an accomplice than the killer.

Deputy Sheriff Jason Lazenby and Investigator Reed inquire of the circumstances of the death of Enright and Grigori discloses the specific circumstances of using the cutter on a dredging boat and the death of Terriff by freezing and feeding to alligators.

With the confession in hand, prosecutors had enough of a case with the recent articles of gene-shaping and accumulated evidence that Seve was gene-shaped to have him arrested on charges of murder and mayhem.

Though the Arc of Tranquility was supposed to make him a national celebrity, the murders made him only a national pariah for being added to the list of GSPs that committed psychotic violent behavior. Seve was later convicted of first degree murder and is on death row exhausting all appeals before he meets the day of his lethal injection.

For his repentance, Grigori was sentenced to life imprisonment because of his favorable testimony.

CHAPTER FIFTY-ONE

Enbryo's Exit

Enbryo was in the forefront of technological advances in gene shaping. There was no question it had augured in a new era of genetic coding and matching that pushed the limits of baby designing to a new level. No one was faulting them for those advances. It was conceivable that experimenting with nature could deliver consequences unpredictable and unforeseeable. Other than the psychotic violent behavior, which was enough for most, the genetic results did reap beautiful and intelligent people that left most in the eugenics field impressed. But the 87.2 % criminal infliction rate was non-negotiable.

It had changed the landscape so diversely. Women who may have had a physical attraction to a man or a woman would intentionally avoid them completely. To be beautiful was no longer the social craving. Just to be average was now the postulate of the day. It was a difficult change in something that was purely biological and hormonally controlled. It was like looking at a banana split or smelling a hot sizzling cinnamon apple crumb pie and shying away from it altogether though every hankering of your constitution pined for it. A majority of women did not even want to embellish their looks for fear that they would be confronted or marginalized in a social gathering. They would go "au natural" without makeup, lipstick, rouge, eyeliner, eye shadow, hair extensions. Some refused to shave their legs and armpits.

It worked into men too. Seduction by either sex took a

nasty turn, when a douse of realism swept into flirtation and courtship. Young people had to accept on terms less than infatuation. Seeing people in their natural element, unaided by beauty aids that highlight features, takes the filter off the illusion. The minds and perceptions of either or both sex, intersex, or non-sex are disheartened by the reality of being just ordinary humans.

Men would see a beautiful woman and would have a strong hormonal hunger for that woman but would have to sidestep the drive and monastically retreat. In some instances, the woman would be the aggressor in initiating the contact. The woman would ask the man or woman out for lunch or a date, and the response would generally be "no" or non-responsive. Some men with a much larger playing field of acceptable beauty would even beg off any contact with someone they regarded as on the fence "beautiful" for fear that it was a GSP.

Cosmetic companies felt the pain too. Fewer products were being sold and beauty was taking a second seat to social survival. A lot of beauty products was not being pushed except to the older folks; those outside the danger zone of youthful psychosis. Advertising came to a standstill when beautiful was not shown or exhibited. Not that ugly was in, but downplaying "good looks" was the acceptable norm.

The litigation absorbed most of the tangible assets of Enbyro and the remaining assets it had were sold and placed into a trust, along with insurance proceeds. This would allow funds to be made available to GSPs and victims who were harmed by Enbyro's failure to notify and promptly take steps to protect the general public. Dr. Marjorie Birmbaum retired and sought exile in a remote part of Northern Canada away from media cameras and coverage. She regrets the steps she took to conceal the results of the study. One District Attorney is contemplating filing criminal charges against her for that failure to notify. Others have thought that even if she delayed in responding to the proclivity of GSPs to commit heinous acts may not have been enough to quell the violent acts. It is always true that the study did not entail whether the propensity to commit violent acts would necessarily adduce to committing those acts in real time. For that reason, in and of itself, many District Attorneys and City Attorneys passed on prosecuting Birmbaum on the concealment of the study.

CHAPTER FIFTY-TWO

Away Without Leave

For three days and nights in a row, Sabrina had Glen tangled up in love-making that was endless. It routinely started with denatured balm, then DTM, a little hypnotic suggestion, and then wild forays into the world of exotic pleasures. When she had Glen and Jan at the massage salon it was just an hour or so of DTM. But at her home, the brainwashing became so effective and intense. Glen was too far gone to be concerned about news reports on GSP's and to have any suspicions about Sabrina being a GSP. He felt, at all times, it was true love. The 50-60 years difference in age was meaningless to him and he willingly surrendered himself to her.

Through hypnotic suggestion, he had all but forgot Jan. The incantations of Sabrina as the high priestess had a lot to do with it, saying, "Sabrina is yours to have and to hold," "love me with all your heart," "I'm yours." Those would be the typical words of a lover trying to win the heart of another. But deep in the brain, hidden in some recess of a remote sulcus, there was something more minatory stewing. Sabrina had the dark thoughts in the past but her ingenuity always got the best of her in finding solutions no matter how evil. "I need to assure his net worth remains at $225 million. If Jan gets a large part of the estate, I will get next to nothing should I try to inherit from Glen's estate." Sabrina Zablowsky had already married Glen in her mind before the divorce papers were ever filed. Thinking out loud, "if he goes through divorce, it may take 4-5 years before the marital estate is resolved. Given his many assets, it could even take longer. That means, he could be 90 years of age before the marriage is terminated and community property divided up. That's too long to wait. What happens if he dies during the dissolution of marriage, I can't marry him until he is divorced. If he dies, most of the assets will go to Jan and/or his next of kin. I need to eliminate her from the equation. If she is dead, there is no divorce and I can marry Glen immediately and have him change his will to assure I get the bulk of his estate. I'll be a millionaire at the young age of 25 years. Now, how can I hatch this plot."

If she uses "killing" as part of the hypnotic suggestion, it could implicate her in Jan's death should Glen relapse to his former self. She thinks, "I still have access to Jan."

Sabrina calls Jan later that day. "How are you doing? Have not seen you in a while." Jan sounds depressed. "Glen did not come home in the last three days. I don't know where he has gone. I'm concerned." Sabrina tells Jan, "I just saw him recently and he said he would be coming home today." Jan asks, "did he come into your salon?" Hazily, Sabrina answers, "I believe he did." Jan inquires, "did he ask about me?" "No, he didn't," says Sabrina, adding, "he must have his mind on other things. Would you like to come in for a massage today? It's on me." Somewhat reticent at the overture, Jan answers, "okay."

Sabrina's approach with Jan is distinctly different from earlier massages. She applies the denatured balm but omits the hypnotic suggestion. She thinks, "I can easily manipulate her into a very depressed state where suicide is the only option but that may come back to haunt me. But there are other ways to achieve victory here. I have a holistic friend from China that uses herbal bags of tea for euthanasia benefits. Along with herbal tea the bag contains ricin that delivers a poisonous dose to one's life." She acquired the tea bags at a conference years ago in Beijing and held on to it for just this reason.

While Jan is in a semi-conscious state, with rubber gloves on, Sabrina places the tea bag with its envelope in Jan's purse. After the massage is over and Jan regains full awareness, Sabrina says, "I looked through your purse, Jan, and I saw a tea bag in it that had not been used. That tea bag may help you with the bundle of emotions you're feeling with Glen being absent from the home." Jan retorts, "I was unaware it was in there, but my mind is slipping these days. I'm ready for tea. I'll have it when I get home." Jan hobbles out the door of the salon. Sabrina believes she is closer to victory than any other time in her life. She smiles contently.

Just as she said she would, Jan returns home and the very first thing she does is put a pot of water on the stove and heats it to a boil. After steeping the tea bag in the cup of hot water, Jan drinks it down. Her purse is on the table next where the tea is drunk.

Later that day, around 7 in the evening, Glen enters the home to find Jan's head face down on the table. Glen says, "Jan, Jan, are you alright?" But there is no reaction. He checks her heartbeat and finds that it has stopped. He calls emergency medical response and they arrive at the residence several minutes later and pronounce Jan dead at the scene. Ricin poisoning is not contagious and cannot be spread from person to person through casual contact, so Glen did not have any exposure to it that would have any lethal consequence. Glen is in a state of shock, remorseful and now feeling that his cheating on his wife was wrong. "Why did I do this? My wife who loved me would not have committed suicide had I been at the home and not away for three days." Grief-stricken he sits in the kitchen as police investigators sift through any evidence that would establish there was foul play. He is so sad that their relationship ended in this way. They had planned for a future together that would continue until the last dying ember of their lives burnt out. Finding his wife dead on the kitchen table is not something he would ever imagine occurring. He is overcome with grief.

CHAPTER FIFTY-THREE

Filling The Void

Obsessed with finding out the results, Sabrina hurries by the Glen and Jan's residence and sees the coroner's office and local police department detectives there. She refuses to call Glen until they are all gone. She makes periodic trips by the home and, by sundown, the investigation has ceased. Sabrina thinks, "did I leave any trace of evidence that Jan was here at the salon today? I did call her before she died, so I will be on the list of potential witnesses."

She was just about ready to call Glen and then a call comes in from the police department. "Hi, this is Detective Gonzales. I would like to come by and speak with you." Nervously, Sabrina asks, "What is it about?" Not disclosing too much, "I can't say but we are investigating a potential homicide," states the Detective. He continues, "can I come by in a quarter of an hour?" Sabrina answers, "yes."

At the appointed time, Detective Gonzales enters Sabrina's salon announcing, "I am Det. Gonzales of the police department. And you are?" She answers, "Sabrina Zablowsky." He inquires, "is this your salon?" "Yes," she answers. "Nice place. This is where you do massages?" he asks. "Yes," Sabrina says keeping her answers short and to the point. "I understand that Jan and Glen Pridley came here for massages." "Yes. They are my business patrons," replies Sabrina. "Is this where you massaged them?" he asks.

"Yes," is her reply. He looks around the massage area and notices a lot of Chinese artwork and objects d'art. "I see you like Chinese themes," he propounds. "Yes. It relaxes those being massaged." He inquires, "when were you in China last?" Sabrina answers, "three years ago." "Did you bring home anything on that trip?" questions the Detective. "Just artwork. Nothing else." He then asks: "Cell phone records show that about 5 hours ago you called Jan Pridley. Is that correct?" Sabrina replies, "I was simply following up with her about her depressed state and thought that, maybe, she would benefit with a massage." "What did she say to you? asks the Detective. "Her words were, 'a massage won't make me feel better. I'm too depressed. I'm gonna stay home,'" quotes Sabrina. "When was the last time you saw Jan?" asks Detective Gonzales. "Let me look at my calendar." Going through the calendar, she answers, "15 days ago." "So, more than two weeks ago, you saw Jan," Gonzales concludes. "Yes," says Sabrina.

Then, out of left field, the Detective asks, "weren't you having an affair with her husband Glen?" That remark causes Sabrina to falter a bit and she sits down in a chair near the Detective. "What was it you asked me?" Sabrina asks again. "Didn't you have sexual relations with Glen for three days prior to her death?" Her initial reaction was "I don't know." Then, she states, "that's a private matter." "Ma'am, this is an investigation; not a custodial interrogation," he comments." "Do you want to hinder this investigation by asserting your right of privacy? It doesn't really matter because Glen has told us, waiving his right of privacy, that he had three days of sex with you and went home the third day to find his wife dead at the kitchen table." Realizing that if Glen waives the privacy, there was nothing to hide, Sabrina answers, "Yes, we had sex for three days." "Do you believe that Jan was depressed because her husband was cheating with you?" Detective asks. "I really don't know the inner workings of that family. I was just their massage therapist," she answers. "Do you have anything else to add?" finishes the Detective, "No," she replies.

As soon as the Detective leaves, Sabrina thinks, "I can't stay. I've got to get out of here before they focus on me." Sabrina, within the matter of two hours, has everything packed and in her car. She is running from the law. "I've got to lose myself in the countryside and wait it out," she decides. One of her friends suggested a certain place that enforcement doesn't go as the best place to hide.

Sabrina found the secluded place upslope from a river and thought, "Gee, this is off the beaten path. I should be safe here. I'll sleep in my car at night for security." On the second night in this location, Sabrina falls asleep on the slope. Something disturbs her sleep and she sees a dark creature approaching her. She wakes up and starts running for her car. When she arrives at the car, she looks back and sees the mysterious creature approaching her. She steps into the car and locks the door. She looks on in fright as the creature wields his axe into the window shattering it into many pieces. Sabrina crosses the console and finds refuge on the passenger side. Raising her hands to protect herself from the advances of this monster, he swipes at her hands severing them from her arms and forearms. Sabrina goes into shock and begins to kick with her feet. His mighty axe cuts her legs off at the knees and she now has no defense. Pain is the total experience. The mysterious man, Gizpaco, comes into view and he grabs her thighs and pulls her out of the car through the broken window. When she is on the ground outside the car, he asks, "I will take you to paradise." With that, his axe separates her head from her body and she dies instantly. Her eyes blink several times before coming to rest wide open. He removes both of her eyes and other body parts. Once the operation is concluded, he places Sabrina in a body bag and takes her down the river to her final resting place. As he maneuvers the gondola down the river, this night, he sings a song, "sins can be forever washed in the river of life. When our life ends, the soul will rise."

CHAPTER FIFTY-FOUR

Affluence Of Dia's Influence

Both Eadred and Sierra are terribly concerned about their daughter Dia. She no longer needs their support and is living in a mansion in St. Petersburg, Florida and has condominiums in New York and Los Angeles. This new-found wealth had all been acquired before she barely reached her 20th birthday. Sierra states to Eadred, "she must be doing drugs. How does someone amass such a fortune in 1-2 years?" Eadred comes to her defense stating, "she is an attractive girl with a large brain in her head. She's gifted. We knew that going in." Sierra adds, "she is so secretive about what she does. It almost seems criminal. She said she is in body procurement. What does that mean?" Eadred quips, "she's making a living. That's all that matters."

Dia meets Gizpaco on a deserted road some distance away from the river and the bridge. She has been doing this for the length of her involvement in procurement. His presence in an urban setting would draw too much attention. When they meet it is close to dark and Gizpaco hands a plastic container to Dia, saying, "eyeballs." He hands a black bag to her and states, "entrails and limbs." Dia hands cash to Gizpaco and says, "thank you." That was the typical encounter between Dia and Gizpaco; never more than a few words. Dia starts to walk away and Gizpaco adds: "Are you ready for salvation?" Dia replies, "as you when my life ends." "Do you know when your life will end?" "No," answers Dia. She adds, "why do you ask?" Gizpaco states, "we must all be ready for our last day." Dia responds, "I'm sure that when it is my last day, I'll be ready." "Have you repented?"

he probes. Dia retorts, "what's there to repent?" "Your sins," he answers. Dia responds, "I don't have a guilty conscience, so I have not sinned." "You have not sinned?" asks Gizpaco. "No," is the quick reply of Dia. Then, at a moment of heightened tension, certainly driven by her immaturity, she says the wrong thing: "You're the one that's killing these people, not me." Gizpaco does not respond to that inconsiderate remark, only grumbles, then walks away disappearing into darkness.

When she returns home, she receives a call from the actual celebrity who states, "I really enjoy my eye. You have saved me. But my balance is off and I need a second eye. I have stumbled on stage trying to get a 2-dimensional perspective on the stage floor and standing on objects. What are the chances of getting a second eye?" Dia responds, "I am a great fan of yours and have listened to your music over the years. I have received a legacy of two eyes just recently but they have been purchased by a sheik in the middle east so they are unavailable. I can try to locate one." The celebrity notes, "one that is blue so it matches the other eye. I am willing to pay $4 million for the eye." Dia laughingly states, "that will definitely arouse my interest to find the matching eye. I'll keep in touch."

CHAPTER FIFTY-FIVE

Vaping

Samantha looks in the mirror of her bathroom and role-plays how she is going to walk out of this place never to return. She thinks, "Rebecca's death was ruled a suicide so they have nothing on me. I'm free to go and live elsewhere. The hell with this mansion and this guy's money. I'm out the door." She looks around for the "under woman" outfit and cannot find it or any other garment in the closet or in the dresser drawers. "Damn. He is always playing these fuckin" games. I'm going down there and give him my piece of mind. Should I wrap a towel around me? No. He's got cameras in this room and has seen me nude many times in a state of undress." Not thinking it through, she does just that. She marches downstairs to confront Algar. There is some music playing in the library where he is seated. Samantha comes over to Algar and says, "this is all wrong." Algar extends his hands as if he wants to dance. A little unsure of what to do, she thinks, "wait a minute. Maybe this guy is beginning to see me in all my beauty. Love might be abounding. Let's see what happens with the dance." She clasps his hands and they begin to dance in less than fundamental ways with Samantha's steps much longer and her gait wider than Algar's. She smiles back at Algar and thinks, "this isn't so bad. Maybe we just needed to dance to clear the air." Seeing Samantha totally naked, Algar grabs her right breast and she does not refuse but kind of pushes his left hand away. She laughs indicating she was not opposed to the contact. "I don't want to give him too much contact or he may lose interest. This is all part of the subjugation of the male, no matter what their age." Dancing goes on for another 10 minutes and after its concluded, Samantha says, "I'll make us breakfast." She runs off to the kitchen and pans start banging and Samantha places an apron over her pubic area, leaving the top exposed.

When breakfast is ready, Algar comes in and Samantha takes the apron off and they both have a breakfast of oatmeal, chicken bacon, and scrambled eggs with cheese.

Apparently, a corporate monitor saw the dancing and reported it to the local authorities. Officers Al Williams and Sam Cunningham knock on the door of the manor. Samantha comes to the door with a bed sheet wrapped around her. "Ma'am, we have had reports that you are naked in the presence of a minor. Is that correct?" She replies, "they took my clothes. I have nothing to wear. I have to roam around here naked." Officer Williams replies, "we are just warning you this time to wear clothes in the presence of the minor. If you don't have clothes, buy clothes and wear them around the house. Otherwise, we have to arrest you for indecent exposure." Not wanting to fight it out at the threshold of the door, Samantha agrees and says, "I will wear clothes." She shuts the door.

Angry at what has taken place, she approaches Algar, "I need clothes. Not children's costumes. I'm a woman and must dress like a woman. Buy me some clothes and now." The angry look on Samantha's face does little to cause any reaction. Out of the blue he states, "do you vape?" She answers, "no, I don't and I never will. These lungs have never inhaled polluted air, cigarette smoke, cigar smoke, or any smoke whatsoever." Algar asks, "how about fire smoke?" "No, not even that," she replies.

"The officers said, 'you shouldn't be naked in front of me.' Then, you ask me to buy you clothes," says Algar, handing the vape gun to Samantha and says, "for your punishment, smoke." "No, I'm not smoking that," she replies. "Smoke or be arrested," he gives his ultimatum. She thinks, "he's got me dancing with him naked and the police know about it. I could be easily accused of indecent exposure and child molestation." Realizing the cards are stacked against her, she grabs the vape gun and slightly inhales the smoke. She coughs a little and continues to smoke. The peach flavored scent has some appeal to her and she draws more deeply on the mouthpiece. The vape oil has a sedative property in it which causes Samantha to get tired and she decides to go up to bed and sleep it off.

The sedation is so strong that she sleeps not knowing that the vape gun is in her mouth. As she breathes in and out, she is inhaling a large volume of smoke. She occasionally coughs. Her sleep is so deep and coma-like, it is not interrupted by the coughing. After 5 hours, Samantha wakes up from the sleep, coughing excessively and throws the vape gun against the wall. She is experiencing a coughing spasm and runs to the bathroom. She looks at her face and it appears gaunt. She turns on the water and flushes her face with hot water. The cough is persistent for about 3 hours and begins to wear off. Still naked, she doesn't seem to care what the officers said and she goes to the kitchen to get some food. Algar is nowhere to be seen. Her lungs seem to be filled with smoke and she takes deep breaths to free her lungs of that pollutant. She is mad at Algar, but, rather than to confront him, she has decided to leave him and this mansion of death. She grabs a towel and two belts and fastens one belt to the top of the towel and a belt to the lower extremities of the towel so that she will have coverage from exposing herself. She exits the house and starts walking down the long driveway to the street. She has no money, no clothes and nothing of value on her person. She sees the gate's entrance not far from where she is at and feels the surge of freedom close at hand. She quickens her steps toward the gate. Suddenly, from a pen obscured in a cluster of trees, two black rottweilers appear racing toward Samantha. Samantha cries out, "oh my God. I didn't know he had dogs." She begins to run toward the gate. The dogs are closing in on Samantha. She stumbles but regains her balance. She is just 50 feet from the gate when the first dog grabs her right leg causing her to fall. She strikes at the first dog as the second dog latches onto her neck. She uses her hands to try to free the dog's bite around her neck. The dog's bite is overpowering and pierces the jugular vein. Bleeding to death, Samantha eventually loses consciousness and then dies. Algar, stationed in front of a camera display, sees the encounter and that Samantha dies from his dogs' clashes with her. He looks up and smiles at the result.

CHAPTER FIFTY-SIX

Famous Final Scene

Dia meets Gizpaco on the same deserted road. She is excited about the prospects of earning $4 million to obtain a blue eye. She knows it can be done; it's been done in the past. Today, there is a change in the air. This time Dia offers more information about the request for the eye. "Gizpaco, I need a blue eye for this celebrity. She is a talented stage performer named Solace Beganti. Her balance on stage is affected by only having one good eye. She needs a second. Find a blue eye and we will be in business. She is willing to pay $4 million for the eye."

Gizpaco heard the backstory but doesn't seem to be interested in the subject content. He stares closely into Dia's eyes and states, "have you repented for your sins?" Dia retorts, "we have been through this the last time. I have nothing to repent. I have not sinned. You have. You need to repent." Gizpaco answers, "I have repented and asked for forgiveness." "Good, she exclaims, "then you are good to go." She continues, "I can't babysit this or handle your feelings towards salvation. That's for you to earn. Mine, right now, is to deliver one blue eye. Got it."

Dia turns to walk away and Gizpaco takes his axe and hatchets Dia in the back. She looks at him bewildered. She falls to the ground when the axe splits her spinal cord into two. "Don't do this," as she pleads for her life. "Did you repent? Salvation is near," says Gizpaco. Dia cannot talk now. Her body is shutting down. He takes her body and places it in the gondola face up. The pain is gone as Dia looks up at the stars. She feels the warm blood exiting her body and her strength melting away with each breath she takes. She feels the cool of the night wafting over her face. He takes her on the moonlit night on her last stroll down the river of life. The Moon shines a gold aura over the boat and Dia. Gizpaco sings a song, "sins can be forever washed in the river of life. When our life ends, the soul will rise." He periodically stops to pick up body bags that begin to fill the gondola. Looking straight up into the starry night, Dia is still alive and hearing the song sung by Gizpaco.

When they arrive to the Trafalgar Bridge, Gizpaco carries Dia, still alive, to the oily tar pond near the Bridge. He raises her body up and then announces, "the soul will rise." He heaves Dia into the pond and she disappears into the ooze forever.

Sensing his work is done, Gizpaco walks up and onto the Trafalgar Bridge, and, only in the presence of brilliant moonlight, he raises his hands to the heavens and says, "free my soul from this imperfect body." He then dives into the oily pond and sinks in the muck to its bottom.

THE END

ACKNOWLEDGEMENT

Roger McCaffrey is a dear friend of the Author and a fellow attorney and basketball player. He is an avid reader. You will never meet him unless he has a book in his hand. Roger has been used by the Author as a sounding board for a few of his literary projects. A recent screenplay called "LowBottomMe" originated from an idea that was discussed during one of Author's many lunches with McCaffrey.

Author wishes to thank Roger for his friendship and companionship over the years as a professional, as a fellow basketball player and as a executive board member of FIOLA ("French-Irish Organization of Lawyers of America").

ABOUT THE AUTHOR

Dale M. Fiola

Fiola has written 11 screenplays and 6 musicals. He has recently released a movie called "Caralique." It is a story about a child prodigy, who becomes the new Coco Chanel. Caralique has won several film festivals awards. It was written for general audiences.

BOOKS BY THIS AUTHOR

The Devalued

The world is tied to the internet through cerebral implanting. Though each implanted has access to all the information that the internet holds, the internet knows most everything about the implanted, including his/her innermost thoughts. The unimplanted rebel.

BOOKS BY THIS AUTHOR

Al-Law-Gory

A tale about a retired judge handling capital cases in Idaho. His decisions are countermanded by Valkyries who have taken over the old Courthouse. The Judge has his own perceptions of the guilt or innocence of an accused based upon limited information. However, the Valkyries know the inside story on each and dispense justice in their own designated, horrific ways.